~~THE EMPATH SERIES~~

I0545006

THE GATES OF ATHENA

~ BOOK I ~

CAROLE RAMSAY

Stereo A Typical Press

STEREO-A-TYPICAL PRESS
Denver, Colorado
Stereoatypicalpress.com

September 2017

ISBN: 9781946293022

COVER ART BY:
TORY TOMKIEWICZ

Printed in the United States of America

PUBLISHER'S NOTE
This is a work of fiction. Names, characters, places, and incidents either are the product of the author's imagination or are used fictitiously, and any resemblance to actual persons, living or dead, events, or locales is entirely coincidental.

For David

for Malcolm, Danielle,
Chloe, Tory, Bradley and Bella

PROLOGUE

The beautiful Dr. Orlean, tall and raven-haired, stood at the top of her mountain camp. Hundreds of others, saved by the good doctor when she had offered them refuge beyond her Gates, went about their business in the many buildings and meadows behind her. Standing cliff side in the direction opposite them, she breathed in, slowly, deeply. Then she raised her arms out to her sides, closed her eyes, and leaned slightly in, toward the valley floor far below her. All the while, the sun scorched down and the wind howled fiercely in a westerly direction.

Carried on Second-Sight, a series of visions in rapid succession filled Dr. Anna's mind. As if the first slide in a show, a herd of now-wild horses galloped, hard and fast, in a meadow quite familiar to her.

Suddenly, she saw instead, a very large man, one eye injured, sitting on a bed. This man wore an orange coverall garment, had darkened skin and was reading a book, *the Dhammapada,* while he mumbled a chant. Quickly then, her vision became one of a white-capped body of water. It was a body of water high above the building where the man in orange sat. A dam held back this body of water in the vision, but it seemed, only just barely. Rapidly, the mental slide-show shifted to an area below the building in the opposite direction, and showed her a tall, thin and red figure peeking into a convention center building. She knew that red statue too. Called, *The Alien,* it was flagship artwork for the city of Distoria.

She saw the full moon then, sitting, beautiful and unaffected, far above all this. Her vision focused more closely on the moon, as if zooming in on it, and she saw the Moon Station upon its surface, and people determinedly moving about inside it. The vision moved away from the moon's surface and out into space where Dr. Orlean next saw a space station. It was station ISO#V1.0651. More populous than many earth cities and known affectionately as, *Babylon*, it was one hundred and forty-seven floors of constant action.

On one of the floors, at a loading zone, a bus docked beside the station, hovering while species of being of every color, size and manner unloaded into the Station. When it was emptied, many more including a human bound for Earth, boarded the same bus which, moments later, departed.

In her slide-show, it was less than a second later when that bus unloaded at its destination. The human disembarked on Earth, walked passed the prison wherein the large man sat reading, then passed many large fans on the sidewalk, then passed a child who, though surrounded by people, stood speaking to no one in particular. The child was saying something that was, to Anna, seemingly obvious, *Your violence will stop you,* he said.

Suddenly the scene changed though as the three young men nearest the child, moved in closer to him. Two of them then punched him hard before passersby jumped in and pulled the young men from the boy. Anna now knew why this vision had been sent. She would need to get the boy, and soon, before The Great Departure when she and those in her camp would leave earth far behind them forever.

The passersby exchanged words with the young men, though Anna, in her vision, did not hear their words. While they spoke, the boy, unseen by them, began to change. First his body became translucent, the light from behind him flickering in and out, and then he disappeared completely from the sidewalk beside them. The young men, and the passersby, finally stopped speaking for a moment, and looked around for the boy.

At the top of the mountain, face sun-burnt and hair in the wind, Dr. Anna's eyes bolted open wide in alarm. She gasped and coughed, pulling hard for air as her arms lowered quickly toward her chest.

1

The young mother walking ahead of Dr. Anna Orlean was far more distracted than was normal for her. She had just exited the bank where her business had not gone as she had hoped and now, on top of that, the baby strapped snugly to her chest in his baby carrier, was crying. In each of her hands she held the hand of one of her two older babies, now toddlers.

Dr. Orlean, sensing the bank trouble as well as other struggles within the woman in front of her, looked up from the headline on her phone, *Violence Against Messengers Grows,* and sent a wordless message of quiet serenity to the young mom. For a moment, the woman walking wondered from where the sudden warmth and peace she felt, had arisen. But then, Peter, at five years old her eldest, happened to catch sight of a delightfully bright-colored remnant of plastic toy on the sidewalk, and he pulled free of his mother's grasp. The moment had passed, and with it the warm feeling passed too, and the woman picked up her pace again, even as she called back to her son to keep up and move along.

Dr. Orlean walked along behind, one eye on the university coming into view on her left, and the other eye squarely on little Peter to her right. She walked passed the enormous fan turning loudly on the sidewalk beside her, then passed a man whose tablet headline read, *Empath Intolerance Increasing,* and kept moving. Every nerve ending in Anna's body was coiled and ready for what she already knew was coming.

At the light, the frazzled young woman, still working to quiet the screaming baby, stepped into the crosswalk and crossed over to the sidewalk on the other side of the street. Five steps behind her, Peter, carrying the bright bits of glued paper and plastic he'd found, stepped into the same crosswalk, unaware that the light had changed and that cars now were moving.

Anna's nerve endings uncoiled and they propelled her forward, springing her into the necessary action. In a single motion, far too fast to register in human scales of time or space, Anna had leapt. Landing beside the boy, she wrapped an arm around him and leapt *again*. Carrying him forward in that single leap, over two moving automobiles, she landed safely on the far sidewalk. She set the boy down behind his mother and walked forward into the crowd and the shops and the maze of the city's alleys before anyone could blink, let alone see her.

Had any human eye or mind registered the action it would have looked like all that had occurred was that a female version of Jack's beanstalk giant had taken one long step forward, followed by a similarly long second step. Just two simple steps, such had been the fluidity of her actions.

The drivers, having stopped without knowing why, now remained stopped. The two drivers continued looking around themselves, searching for information, reasons, answers.

The young mother, none the wiser and still blissfully unaware that her little Peter had ever been in any danger, turned at that moment and saw her son sitting on the damp and dirty sidewalk. Her other child's hand still in her own and the baby now sleeping, the woman called to her son to stop playing in the grimy filth and try to keep up. The boy stood and ran after his mother whose mind was thinking forward to the several more errands she had yet to run on this hot and humid morning.

For her part, Dr. Anna Orlean, who was expected in the larger of the lecture halls at the university across the street, doubled back around the block and crossed over toward her own appointment. Though her legs were as normal in length as those of any human, each of her steps covered the length of a city block.

She walked into the full auditorium to begin addressing the hall of waiting academics, precisely on time.

2

The heat inside the auditorium could easily overwhelm the most enduring of those seated there despite the enormous fans and air conditioning units which had been placed during construction long ago. A banner hung limply across the top of the stage toward the back and it caught Anna's eye as she walked to her seat. *International Anthropological Society* read the top line. Below it was the semi-circular logo, *Conference 2084.* Another large logo took up the front side of the podium and announced Antesapiana College as the location of the sweltering auditorium.

Anna looked at the older professor beside her on the panel and noted the drops of moisture slipping from his face onto his notecards in front of him. He, like all other humans, had seventy years to adjust to the more than seven degree increase in the temperature of the planet, but Anna didn't blame him. In evolutionary terms, she knew, seventy years wasn't even a blip.

The only humans, in fact, who were doing well seemed to be those on the autism spectrum who started appearing in larger, and at the time, confusing, numbers in the late nineteen-hundreds – about twenty years before the start of the planetary temperature shift.

Anna, at her school for them, had predicted this early in her career, having noted the way the students tended to clump near sources of heat. Parents too, related to her, how "*normal*" seemed the behavior of the children when those children were experiencing fevers. Clearly it had been a genetic evolution preparing members of the species for the coming shift.

That topic, though, interesting and controversial as it may be, was not what Dr. Orlean was here to discuss today. Today she had been asked to present, as key note speaker, a different one of her medical anthropological theories. Today's slide show would illustrate for her audience, who had largely attended for this sole reason, how very wrong previous interpretations of gender-based divisions of labor had been a hundred years ago. Today's presentation described further how only extremely rich, decadent, indulgent kinds of societies could afford to sideline half of their talent pool for or from any individual category of labor – and that there had thus far, been no societies which had been sufficiently provided for, sufficiently *rich*, to have fully divided labor in this manner.

On her cue, Anna stood and moved to the podium. The lights went down and her slide show began. With pictures that included female hunters and male gatherers, she illustrated how new evidence indicated clearly that the talents of all were always used in the ways most suited to those talents, on an individual level, and that no society in the history of humanity had ever been rich enough *not* to use valuable talents where they are found, in *whomever* they were found.

"A mutation for instance, allowing improved sight for motion, if found in a female, would have been utilized for hunting, not for gathering. The society wouldn't have been able to afford to overlook such an important skill and genetic improvement. Ten to thirty percent of hunters in these early societies, were female, we now know," Dr. Orlean informed her audience.

"The same," she told them, "has always been true about gatherers as well. An eye for detail, so important in discriminating dangerous plants from edible, would not have been left behind simply because it was borne by a male. Bias," she said pointing her laser pointer at a slide depicting an inadvertent poisoning, "is expensive."

"Societies that rich don't yet exist, not on this planet anyway," Dr. Orlean concluded to rousing applause as audience members got to their feet.

Anna removed the microphone clipped to the front of her blouse and exited the stage. Behind her, she heard the moderator thank her, repeat her name, and move on to other conference business.

At the same moment, a hundred miles away, in the city of Distoria, angry, dark, storm-whipped water edged closer to breeching the dam that held it. Smashing into the wall of the dam over and over, white-capped and frenzied, the water seemed nearly alive, so driven to find its exit was it, so driven to find its way downhill and toward the ocean. The vulnerable Distoria beyond the dam lay innocent and inattentive, in stark contrast to the turbulent water. Neither the twenty-five-foot red alien statue that peered in, zoo-like, on the people of the convention center, nor the alarm in Dr. Anna's school which would sound when the water breeched the dam, had yet been affected by the water's seeming anger.

In the hallway behind the stage at the conference, Anna turned left to head toward the Medical Center portion of the building. After that first hallway, she looked around, and seeing no one, she stepped forward with one leg, and this time, the step stretched to the end of the hallway. Catching up to her first leg with her second, she now stood at the end of the second hallway. Though she didn't need them, there were signs at the end of this second hallway, indicating the medical center and robotics and physics labs to her right, and her school to her left. She turned right, nodded hello to a few passing colleagues as she walked, and turned in again at the door labeled with her name.

Inside her office, Anna put on her lab coat and leafed through a few files. She took the files with her as she continued toward the labs.

Miles away in a second direction from the university, the city of Malanthron also lay vulnerable, just as the city of Distoria and even the city of Antesapiana itself, housing the university, did. Each of these cities, surrounded for years by growing, ice-melt-fed oceans, had been long protected by a series of dams. Now however, the water behind each of those dams churned away maniacally, growing increasingly ominous with each passing day. The water at each dam slapped at the reinforced concrete at near breeching levels, the occasional whitecap falling over to the spillway below.

The clock tower of Malanthron stood out tall and recognizable against the horizon. These two cities, along with Antesapiana and its Gondola that marked it like a line to heaven, made a ring of sorts around a distant foothill. On the top of the small mountain, owned, the city-dwellers had always heard, by a reclusive eccentric, there was a large and sprawling campus of buildings, paddocks, corrals, and camp buildings. There was, they had also heard, even a small lake.

In the labs beside the university campus, Dr. Orlean walked passed several teams of scientists working on experiments. In the many rooms and sections of rooms, were a wide-ranging variety of on-going projects, everything from robotics to nano-antiviruses to physics. It was toward this area of the labs Anna was moving. The physics projects focused primarily on two interconnected goals. The first involved the astrophysics-based search to locate a stable wormhole, which, in the lab was referred to as STABE Stairs, or sometimes as simply, a STABE. Anna had little need of this project, but funded it nonetheless.

The second set of projects combined mechanical and fuel engineering with the physics needed to push beyond the Alcubierre Drive and break the human incapacity to travel faster than the speed of light. It was with the lead scientist supervising both sets of projects that Anna was meeting – Dr. Gabrielle Hurtt, "Gabby" to Anna.

"You're right on time. I'll be ready in just… a… minute. And… done," Gabby said, tightening a piece of apparatus with a tool that looked too delicate for the job. "Be sure to record that second set of output from the interferometer before recalibrating," she told the gathered post-docs before heading meaningfully toward a counter covered in an abundance of coffee related matter.

Dr. Orlean asked Gabby about her home gardens as the latter poured herself a generous thermos of coffee.

"The hydroponics studies continue to branch us into some fascinating directions." She took a sip then added, "Some of the hybrid plants are also coming along quite well too, actually," Gabby said as though absentmindedly now contemplating the plants. She took another sip and offered a mug to Anna.

"Tea for me, please. Botany must be a relaxing hobby for a physicist?"

"So much. Hands dirty kind of thing. That and my other hobby – researching archaic and completely useless histories and languages – are all I'm ever doing if you can't find me here," Gabby answered with a laugh. "Always one of the two." She handed Anna her tea.

"It's those gifts, those interests I've come to talk with you about in fact." Anna sipped her tea. But, I should tell you, since we're talking gifts anyway, that you have yet another as well, you know."

"Oh?"

"Mmm, indeed," Anna murmured and sipped at the tea again before continuing. "Things are changing, Gabby, you know this as well as anyone. Frankly, your gifts are needed on my team, and more than you can know, you will benefit from being on that team as well.

Gabby waved vaguely around herself and laughed. "Aren't I already on your team?"

"Joining this team means that very soon you will move away from all of this. Quite far away actually. You would be a key player on this other team, Director of Sciences, in fact – all sciences."

"Something tells me far away will be good, very, *very* soon. I'm not sure why I think that, but I do." she said.

"You would still be working on all of the same projects you work on here, and with all the same equipment, and more, anything at all more that you might want, could ever imagine."

"You had me at, 'Frankly, your gifts are needed…' I'm in!"

"You'll be very glad you are."

"That too, is something I feel certain of… and have no idea why!"

When Anna had left Gabby to her many projects with Faster Than Light, or FTL, technology, she crossed the lobby and headed to the school on the other side of the building. Crossing to this second wing, she first stepped into another, smaller lobby. This one was painted in bright colors and there was a classroom on either side of it. Anna turned in at the classroom to the left.

3

Inside the classroom, a young girl sat at a table with a large sheet of paper and a rainbow of colored pencils spread out before her. The drawing revealed uncanny artistic ability, far beyond that normally associated with a nine-year-old child. The hundred-year-old map behind her on the wall depicted a reality very different from that on the girl's planet.

The coastal land zones on the map had long ago become submerged below the new level of the sea when the ice shelves melted. The Canadian ice shelf had gone first, followed quickly by those in Greenland and Russia. The Filchner-Ronne and the Ross ice shelves were now also nearly gone. As such, the girl's drawing depicted much less land than did the map, and much, much more ocean.

In her artwork, the girl and her friends are happy in the sweltering heat, they are the focus of the drawing. They also float high above the planet. The other people, sketched into the background, are much less happy. Instead, the others she had insightfully drawn, were desperate and even violent toward the happy children.

The girl had no expression on her face while drawing her sophisticated artwork, and her expression shifted not at all when a noise caused her to look up and see Dr. Anna coming toward her.

"Hi, Dr. Anna."

"Hi, Delia, I've missed you, how are you today?"

"Fine. Drawing. See?"

"I do see. It's very good."

"Thank you." The girl continued in her work without pause. "It's me," she pointed, "and my friends from school here."

"You look happy."

"We are."

"Why is everyone else not as happy?"

"They're cranky. They're too hot. No fun."

"There's even less land in your drawing. The future?" Anna asked. Delia nodded.

Dr. Anna paused, then she pointed to the floating children in the picture and spoke in a quieter, more serious tone to the girl.

"You know that they don't know, right?" she asked, drawing out her words, and by extension, their meaning.

"Yes" Delia answered bluntly as she always did. But, frowning after a moment, she spoke again. "What is that like for them, Dr. Anna?" the girl asked.

"The not knowing?"

The girl nodded again and Anna instinctively reached out in protection of the girl, pulling her small head toward her own chest and wrapping both arms around her as if with the sheer force of her will she could keep the sweetness of this girl, the innocence of her, in, and the rest of the world and its reality, out.

"Oh, Delia, I wish I knew. But I don't know, not exactly, not first-hand anyway. I do know that it involves fear though, a great mess of fear like you and I have never known. I do know too, that often that fear comes out looking a *whole* lot, like anger."

"...and violence," the girl added, still frowning.

"...and violence," Anna confirmed.

"Is it true they can't feel knowledge though?" Delia asked.

It was Anna's turn to nod. "And because of that, they can feel none of the connections either." The two sat there, the girl and the woman, and thought about that for a moment, trying to guess at what it might *feel* like to be one brain in the world unconnected from all the others, *unaware even,* that the connections existed.

"They don't know what their brains can do, huh?"

"Nope. They believe, for whatever reason, only in machines and in brains of a mechanical nature. They can't interact with, play with," Anna began, and to make this idea clear to the child, she picked up and pulled into various shapes, a quantity of modeling clay from the art supplies nearby, "time and space the way we can. Because they can't feel the knowledge, they can't feel the connections everywhere - so they end up thinking they are separate from time and space, not the same as it."

"Does that mean they don't know they are connected to the past? Or the future? They don't know how to get to the knowledge?"

"Oh, Dear Delia, they don't even know that there *is* knowledge, or that knowledge is freedom. They don't even have a word for that kind of knowledge. So distant from it are they, that the absence generates physical illness in many who feel that absence. How then could they be quiet enough inside to hear how to access that knowledge?"

"It's cause they're always angry 'bout something." Delia said after a thoughtful pause. She paused again then added, "They called me ... psychic ... when I lived out there. It scared them. *I* scared them. I don't understand though, cause they all know what computers can do. Everybody knows a *human* brain is the strongest computer on the planet."

"You're asking me how come they believe in mechanical brains and not in their own, but Delia, there is no answer for *why*. They simply don't realize. We can do with our minds, what they strive to do with machines. *We* can transport through time and through space with only the power of our own human computer brains, stronger than all the mechanical computers on the planet..."

"Combined," the young Delia interjected.

"Combined," Anna acceded. "Either way, they simply don't know they have this tool inside of them, and because they don't know, there is fear. It is a fear from which we are, all of us here, in danger."

"I don't want to be in danger. Is there, will there ever be, any place other than here, at school, where I can be safe, ever?"

"Our world is coming, Dear, our *time* is coming. Soon too, I'd say. I can feel it coming, can't you? Freedom, safety, tolerance, understanding?"

Delia smiled. "And knowledge!"

"And knowledge, Dear." Anna smiled at the girl. "Freedom then, safety. The water rises every day, Delia. Our time of safety is soon, I can feel it."

"I can feel it too, Dr. Anna." Anna gave Delia a hug before rising.

"In the meantime, you'll be coming up to where I go on weekends, my camp. You'll stay there soon, instead of here, until our time comes."

"If that's where you'll be, then I would like that."

"Good!"

The girl returned to her artwork and Anna left the room, waving to Delia from the door. But Delia's focus was once more on her art work.

Anna moved down several more hallways before pushing open an innocuous looking door with a small window in the top half. In the far corner of this room, three students stood directly over the radiator vent. One of these students was rubbing his hands together as if over a campfire. A fourth student lingered close by, staring at the floor and kicking his foot repeatedly. Anna said hello to the students and passed quickly through this room into the next classroom which revealed a second radiator vent, this one with eight students standing around it. Several of those students repeated the hand rubbing behavior of the student in the first classroom.

Anna walked quickly through the room and exited the wing. She returned to her office, picked up her purse, and hung up her lab coat. She exited the hospital and, in the parking lot of the campus, remotely unlocked her car with a beep. Without a hint of the fatigue she should have been experiencing, Anna drove away from her beloved hospital and school for one of the last times.

4

Fifteen minutes later, Anna pulled her car up at a dock at the end of which stood a waiting ferry boat. Minutes after that, Anna stood silhouetted in evening shadows.

Standing on the top deck of the small ferry, she enjoyed the slightly cooler air and the last moments of day light. Unfortunately, this lasted but a moment before a light rain began to drizzle, obscuring Anna's sentimental reflection. Another passenger, watching Anna at that exact point in time, would later swear to his companions that her sudden invisibility was the result of something more than the weather.

When she reappeared below deck at that same moment though, the passenger above was still watching where she had been and not where she had gone, and so had no way to make the connection. The passengers below, crammed in and trying to get out of the rain, didn't register yet another new arrival fleeing the changing weather.

Standing in a tight and hidden corner, Anna shook the water from her hair and headed through the crowd toward the window. As the rain picked up, Anna gazed out at the city now quickly receding from view. Anna, not able to become fatigued in the normal way, remained standing throughout the trip so that others might sit, might rest.

At the next port, Anna left behind the other passengers without chit chat and walked to the small car she kept parked there. She could tell from the puddles in the dirt road that it had rained here too, but it had stopped now and she got into her car dry except for her muddy shoes. She pulled out onto another dirt road and after twenty minutes or so, drove passed several signs announcing, "Private Property" on either side of the road.

Moments later, Anna came to an unassuming, dirt trailhead semi-hidden in the foliage. An Appaloosa stood whinnying at the trail head, having recently arrived herself. Anna smiled and parked. Shasta knew the sound of her car engine. Her whinnying signaled her happiness at Anna's approach. Shasta bounced her head and kicked at the air as Anna parked, then cantered over to the car's open window. She got in close, nestling Anna's shoulder and kissing her until Anna rubbed the horse's ears and scrubbed at her mane. Both parties were clearly happy to see each other after their week apart.

Anna quickly transferred a few things from her car to Shasta's back. Then Anna pulled the barrette from her hair, loosening it to the wind, and threw her right leg over Shasta's back. Her long hair fell around her as Shasta galloped away. Anna hadn't even hit the saddle yet, such was the communication between rider and animal. Anna stood in her stirrups and whooped happily into the night.

It was the next morning before Anna could again see for herself, the vast array of activity that constantly buzzed at her camp. After breakfast, she rode Shasta to a high berm from which she would be able to see most of the camp.

In one area, women and men could be seen, in the early morning light, engaging in sword play. Elsewhere, another group was practicing the art of spear throwing while a third followed behind a large elk herd, hunting together for a single animal that would provide sustenance to the entire camp.

In a clearing, Anna saw the remnants of last night's bonfire surrounded by boulders. She saw the softened grass surrounding it, and knew that a small group would have danced by that firelight, ringed by trees and watched respectfully by many other appreciative campers.

Now, as she watched, a small group of women and men settled into a hillside with their spear-making materials. From the hillside, the group would watch the surrounding area carefully and protectively. At the same time, they would chip away at stones, turning them into spearheads, all the while chatting quietly and amicably, enjoying the day and their work.

Across the meadow beyond the fire pit, many horses roamed free, a small pack of the animals now running in the sunrise. Near them, women and men rode on horseback enjoying the freedom of speed, or for others, it was the peace of an early morning ride. Small cook fires were in evidence throughout the several-hundred-acre camp. Many were being watched by men enjoying their craft, drinking a lightly seasoned malted milk beverage and talking.

Anna turned to her right to take in the beauty of the sun rise reflecting across the high mountain lake. Surrounding the lake, wildflowers were still shaking off the last bits of a light, early season snow. Throughout the acreage and across the camp everywhere, children ran and whooped in their loud and carefree play.

It was a view Anna could never get enough of and felt she could never fully take in. Finally, though, she had to see to other business and, the sun fully risen now, she walked Shasta slowly over to the side of a building that for a camp like this, was oddly modern-looking. To make the building seem even more out of place, a hitching post waited at its front doors. Shasta stopped near it but went her own way once Anna had entered the building.

Hala and Christina, women of thirty-nine and twenty-two years respectively, stood looking out the wide wall of windows across the lobby from where Anna had just entered, their backs to her. Beyond the window, the city of Malanthron could be seen in the far distance, in the valley below the camp. Its clock tower, soaring above the city, stood out among all its landmarks.

Hala was a tall and willowy bio-AI interface. She and Haldor, her counterpart, had been at the camp for several decades – but with Anna for much, much longer. Anna could hear Hala now, explaining a few, often hidden details to her young apprentice.

"All this practicing here, helps each time the Gates open on different eras through history," Hala was saying. "The Gates and to a lesser extent, this camp, exist outside of things like time periods or societal conventions. What Dr. Orlean has done here is to gather together people like me and like you, those of us who can see clearly *through* time, and also through culture and convention."

Hala and Christina turned then, at the noise of footsteps behind them, and both women smiled. "She can tell you herself now. Doctor, how was your travel?"

Anna smiled warmly back. She had missed her friend. "It was very late when I got in last night. My travel was quite untroubled, Dear Hala. I am happy now, to be home again."

"And we are happy to have you back."

"Do you see those people out there, Christina?"

"They look happy."

"They are happy. Here," Anna said. "In their homes though, they were marginalized, ignored, even abused. One result is that many suffered severe and chronic illness. Those who did not, simply stopped trying to contribute to society."

"Society's loss."

"Very much so. Bias, to a society, will always be expensive."

The women continued gazing out the window a moment before Anna remembered the news she had come to tell Hala, "Oh, we've got our Science Director, Hala. Gabby has agreed to join us next weekend. Delia will be up separately as well."

"I'm so pleased. They shall both find good health here, I feel certain. Our explorations will certainly benefit from their skill sets."

"Yes, I hope we can be good for both."

With a nod toward Anna, Hala left them. "Please, Excuse me. Doctor, Christina."

"Of course," Anna said, and she moved away from the windows too. Christina fell in beside her. "Come on, Christina, we have projects to finish before I must go again beyond the Gates come Monday morning."

*

Christina and Dr. Anna walked out together to an exterior pantry shed. Vast quantities of dry goods had been delivered while Anna had been away. They needed now to be stored properly. Stack upon stack of cans in flat boxes surrounded the pantry shed.

Christina had just unloaded a flat of cans onto the shelves when she stepped back to grab another flat and inadvertently caught sight of children in the meadow below. Playing, laughing, riding, and running, the children embodied something for Christina and she caught herself stopping in her tracks to watch. Anna stopped beside her, and in only a moment, both were smiling broadly. Women and men, working together in several small groups, were also laughing as they smoothed spear shafts or chipped arrowheads or harvested produce. Beside the small lake an elk herd gathered, resting and drinking. "That scene, that laughter, captures what this place is all about for me," Christina said. They stood quietly together watching for quite some time.

"Yes, beautiful, isn't it," Anna finally said.

"If only out there, they too knew what was possible," Christina sighed, motioning downhill and beyond the Gates.

"If only," Anna agreed.

"But, Doctor, when Hala refers to the Gates, she mentions... Athena? Why is that, Doctor?

Anna stared out at the expanse a moment longer before speaking.

"You will learn about that very soon, Christina." At length, she turned back to her work. Christina, still curious, followed. Anna started to lift another flat of tins when she stopped a moment. "I don't know about you, but..." and she let her sentence drift off as she closed her eyes and the flats levitated into the shed. Christina did the same and then both women laughed.

5

In a prison, far away, a large African-American man sat in his cell at the edge of his mattress, reading. His face carried a terrible scar. Red and jagged it began above his left eye and continued downward for nearly two full inches. It was of the sort a curved knife would carve out, marking human flesh. The eye itself was occluded a mysterious milky white and lacked all sight.

The book held gently in the man's beefy hands and long fingers was, *The Dhammapada*. He had borrowed this Buddhist text along with the haphazardly piled books at his feet, from the prison library. The authors of the books on the floor included Pema Chodron, Thich Nhat Hanh, Chogram Trungpa, and a list of other famous Buddhist scholars and writers.

A security guard walked along the corridor between cells, loudly calling out to the other inmates on this small wing. He stopped when he got to this man's cell.

"Hey, Tony," the security guard said.

"Hey, Joe," Tony returned.

"Heard your attorneys finally made good."

"Heard that too."

"You leaving us soon then?"

"First thing in the morning, I'm told."

"Other inmates 'round here going to miss you, old man. You've helped a lot of folks here."

Tony barked a humble bark of laughter at that and let his book fall closed, an aspen leaf marking his page.

"That's right funny, isn't it, Joe?" Tony shook his head, "Funny how life goes. Me, a death row inmate helping, someone, anyone...

"An *innocent* death row inmate, and a lot more than one someone."

"Huh." He still couldn't really believe all that was happening. "Me, offering *any*one *anything* at all. Who would have thought it, huh, Joe?"

"Ya, well, they done right by you now. Finally, if you ask me. Took 'em long enough. Glad you're going to get to feel the full sun again, even if it is nearly fatal."

"Ya, that'll feel good, Joe, real good."

Joe gave a nod, quick and short, and resumed his walking. At the next cell, Tony heard Joe start to call out names again. Tony opened his book to the page marked by the leaf and jabbed his huge finger toward a tiny word. Then he looked up again briefly to quietly recite a passage from the text.

"The End-Maker," Joe said, "overpowers the man with attached mind."

He paused, repeated the phrase, paused again and then turned his one good eye back toward the book and continued reading.

6

The sun that Monday morning rose bright and glorious, too bright for most. But Anna, already back in the city at her medical center, enjoyed the way in which the sun rising here was beautiful in a different way than at her camp a hundred miles distant. Both were stunning and, though different, both made her happy and warmed her mentally as well as physically.

She walked along, on the sidewalk, feeling that heat on her back and on her face. She lifted her face up to it even while most others shielded their faces from the now mostly unfiltered nuclear reactor in the sky.

Then, as a young couple, each carrying backpacks, walked toward her, she stopped walking and turned her face full up into the light of the sun. Others stopped then too, as if to look. Still others just walked faster, trying not to make eye contact.

The young man was African-American and Anna knew the young woman to be of Italian heritage. They were students, both eighteen.

Anna smiled then and lowered her face to stare at the pair, her gaze intent but lacking all self-consciousness. She stared and smiled such that the young woman of the couple asked her solicitously if everything was alright, if she were ok.

"Thank you. Yes. I am," Anna answered the girl. To this Anna then added, "You will Pass Through, Deval."

Reassuringly she added, "Both of you, Patrice. Easily. The Gates will be no impediment to you. You will Pass Through. You are… well, some call it blessed. Please, come to the mountain when it is time."

And then, without further interaction or comment, Anna continued walking. Behind her the stunned and bewildered pair stood, unable yet to move. Staring at her, then looking at each other before looking again after Anna's distant figure. They did this over and over.

It was several lengthy minutes after Anna had entered the lobby of her destination before Patrice and Deval, still awed, felt able to move on again.

*

The lobby Anna had entered was appointed every bit as luxuriously as the rest of the decadent high-rise office and condo building around it. Anna's destination was an upper office in this building in the heart of the financial district.

She paused to assess a directory on the lobby wall, along a bank of elevators. Hardwick Hedges and Investments was listed in bold as being on Floors 15-21. Just above it in the list, United First Private Bank was listed as on Floor 24. Anna would need the latter. She pushed the button for the elevator and waited. In a moment, a bell made a high-pitched ding and the elevator doors slid open.

Four men in expensive suits stood talking in the elevator. Clearly, thought Anna, these four were from the first listing, Hardwick Hedges and Investments. "…She was hotter than a smoking...," one of the men was saying before being interrupted by another.

"Not as hot as my new investment product. Made this one so convoluted, even the SEC won't unravel it for years."

"By then, you'll be sitting in paradise kicking back in margarita-ville." At that, all the men stepped out of the elevator laughing ridiculously.

"Hot women lined up in the beach sand for me!"

The men passed by Anna without seeing her.

"You will not pass through. The Gates will prove too challenging, you will not make it," Anna said. She looked straight ahead, into the now-empty elevator, as she spoke.

"You talking to us?" said one of the men, stopping. The rest of the men stopped now too.

"Lady, we've *already* made it," said the one with the new convoluted investment vehicle. His buddies laughed again.

"Not in the ways that matter you haven't," she said before shifting to speak directly to only one. "Grow, William," she said, "You hold within you what is possible. You alone among these."

She was still staring straight ahead. When she finished speaking, she moved to the spot in the elevator where her gaze had pointed. She hit a button and looked at the bewildered men until the doors closed mechanically between her and them.

The men stood there dumbly a moment, staring after her, then blinking, before finally laughing to shake off the experience and moving back into the stream of their day. Though each would try to regain the flow of his day, his week, each would reluctantly flash on this moment in the weeks to come, each time becoming again, disconcerted, dismayed… and deeply afraid.

*

It was only a moment before the doors of the elevator opened again, this time on floor number twenty-four. There, Anna alighted into a hallway leading to the corporate offices of her bank. She turned right and walked down the hallway till she approached a set of glass doors labeled, *United First Private Bank*.

She opened the door and entered a lobby area to be met immediately by the sound of a large but quiet fan. As evidenced by dampened brows throughout the employees in their cubicles, the fan did little to deter the stifling heat of the day, the building, or the bank offices lobby area.

A young man sat at the desk just inside the door. He looked up and immediately recognized his customer.

"Hello, Dr. Orlean!"

"Hello there, John. How have you and your wonderful family been?"

"Fine! Fine, we've been well. Little one due any day now, you know." He stood to walk Anna toward a vice president's office.

"Be sure to head up mountain when the waters come," she said. John laughed a little, and looked questioningly at this always eccentric client.

"I don't think we'll be climbing any mountains when Michelle's water breaks." His laugh was the tiniest bit nervous. "Will we?"

"You'll know. Just head up mountain, o.k.? Michelle will know."

"Will you be closing another account today?" he asked, though his thoughts were still on Anna's words and his smile still reflected the unsettling oddness of those words.

"Indeed."

"It's good you have so many accounts with us or we'd have to call these last few weeks a run on the bank and shut her down!" He said, his fear evident in his overdone laughter.

"Happily, the camp has a lot of new mouths to feed and house."

"The camp. That's what you're doing with all this? I'd love to come see what kind of camp you've got going, Dr. Orlean."

"This is what the money has always been for. When the water comes, John, you will. And, you'll be glad of all these withdrawals and will have all your questions answered, when the water comes."

"I'll just have to trust you on that one, I guess," John said, still utterly perplexed. "But, for now anyway, here you are." They had arrived at the office and the vice president with whom Anna regularly dealt moved from his desk toward his door.

"Just remember to walk *uphill* then. We'll be waiting for you."

"Ok, Dr. Orlean, whatever you say," John humored her with the same smile still on his face as he headed back to his desk by the elevators.

7

That afternoon, Anna left the city. But this time, it was not to head back to camp because tonight she had dinner plans in New York City. She turned left at the first alley from the bank building. The young man selling meth in the alley and his equally young client both stood gape-mouthed at the short, sudden and intense burst of wind that hit the far end of the narrow roadway.

"That was like a damn hurricane or whatever," said the client.

"What happened to that lady though, man?" The seller walked two steps in what had been her direction. Behind him, his customer laughed hard and slapped him on the back.

"Like you da man, right? You a hero now, gonna save her, right, right? Dude, wasn't no woman in this alley no-how."

"Alright already, you don't gotta bust a gut, creepin' Lurper," the seller said, but he too was laughing. The transaction on his mind again, the woman he hadn't been sure was even there, was already long forgotten.

Once she arrived, it wasn't a long walk to her destination at Thirty Rockefeller Plaza, so she ignored the cabs in favor of stretching her legs a bit. As she got closer to her destination though, she noticed a small group milling about outside the building's doors. She continued forward but as she got closer, the group swelled toward her, and in its ebb and flow, engulfed her. It was as if the group's momentum alone carried her along, as on a wave, into the lobby and then, into the elevator.

The adoring group moved with her to the Seventieth floor, toward the man they adored. Once the elevator doors finally opened, the human wave broke, soaking into the hallway.

As the group jostled, excited but unsure of their next move, Anna heard her name being called. She looked up to see a large man moving easily through the crowd, which fell aside almost before his feet as he walked, as if he were parting this sea. He turned each person by their collar and looked into each face as he asked, "Dr. Orlean? Dr. Orlean?" pronouncing it with two syllables as most did, instead of three.

"Here," she said.

But by the time he could hear her over the noise around them, she was the last one still unasked anyway.

"Over here," she said, much louder, wondering not for the first time whether it would have been more sensible to meet her friend at the restaurant *after* his show had finished filming.

"There you are." The large man moved as if to stand her on her feet. Given that she was already standing, he translated his motion into something else that then fell short of its goal. He let the unfinished action hang there. "Come on," he said instead, "follow me, we're late."

He walked with purpose and Anna, dusting herself off, followed. She was aware of powdery, aromatic make-up and of a wide complex of sound following her as they walked. Dozens of large but silent fans contributed to the sense of hyperactivity. Despite them, as always, the heat in the building lingered at oppressive.

"You can wait in here, it's the green room. Usually where the guests wait but David said to let you in." Anna walked passed the man and sat down. "The last segment is nearly finished taping, so you won't have long to wait."

After the door closed behind the man, Anna got herself a bottle of sparkling water and on the room's television screen hanging above the refrigerator, watched her friend finish up. She hadn't finished the bottle of water before David was opening the door. Another man was with him.

*

At the restaurant, their table was ready for them and as they walked that way, it became clear to Anna that both the men she was with were well-known. David's plainclothes security operatives took a table not far from them.

"I've enjoyed seeing the transition to political life you are making from Hollywood, George," David said. Anna deduced that the fifty-something man must be an actor. The conversation moved toward national policy, the heat, and kept moving from there.

*

"That's what I love about this woman," David said, his third glass of wine to his lips. "The rest of us rant amongst ourselves while she's having discussions on foreign policy with the secretary of state? Seriously? No, really, who else do you chat with, Gandhi, Buddha...?" David laughed.

I have had," Anna said, totally unaware of the joking nature of the question, "the honor of meeting President Layburn and his lovely wife."

"Not our strongest presidential representative, eh?"

"I don't know, that all depends on whether you define strength naively or not."

There was a noise and sudden movement at a table several removed from their own. Anna paid it no attention.

"And what, exactly, is a naive definition of strength?"

"I just mean, is strength walking into a room carrying a gun and not being afraid, or is strength the ability to go into the same room without even a shield, despite your fear?"

David was looking at Anna in a way she didn't understand. His mouth was open but, surprising her, he said nothing. She looked around her at the restaurant manager moving rapidly toward that other table while they talked.

"Only the naive fool would champion the former. But if it's sophisticated strength you like, look no further than those gifted souls the press has begun calling the Messengers, and the intolerance toward them. At the center of each of these inhuman attacks is a person of immense strength not allowing him or herself to be defined by the violence." After a moment, David began clapping, George did the same.

*

In the prison in Distoria, the large man named Tony had been quietly sweeping the floor of the prison's media room. He suddenly stopped working and looked up at the caged television on the wall.

*

In the restaurant, Anna's conversation with the actors was forced to a stop. The commotion at the other table had increased. Now two police officers were stepping up to the table. One of them was handcuffing a patron there. One of David's operatives moved to speak with the officers. When he had finished he came over to their table and spoke quietly into David's ear.

"Paparazzi," David said when the operative had returned to his own table. "Seems we already made the entertainment news for the evening. Live feed. *V! Live* via cell phone."

*

In the prison in Distoria, a Guard pushed his foot off the back wall to propel himself forward and walked to the front of the room to stand beside Tony who was now leaning on his broom, listening intently.

When David and then George began slowly but loudly clapping, Tony too clapped slowly, in the prison. Tony also wanted to smile at this woman, but instead only nodded when his friend said, "She something, huh, Tony?"

"Yeah, she something alright, she something," Tony finally said.

"They say just head uphill you want to find her."

"Uphill, huh?" Tony said.

*

"You're leaving?" George asked her. The cell phone using would-be journalist had been taken away and she was standing to go.

"I have a plane to catch."

"That was pretty awesome."

"It was?"

"Yes."

"Oh. Well, thank you then. I really am sorry I can't stay to talk, more especially since you probably don't get out to my part of the country much."

"All the time! I love it there."

"Really, you go there a lot?" Anna asked, looking dubious.

"No. Not at all, I've never been, actually." They both laughed at that. "But now," he said, "I'm sure I'll be there quite a bit, and I'm sure that I will love it."

Anna smiled and turned to go.

"I'll call," he yelled after her.

Anna smiled again at the idea, quite sure that he wouldn't.

"David has my number."

She rode down again in the elevator and exited the building. She walked out into the moonlight on the sidewalk moments later. She moved toward a hotel she knew, where on the seventeenth floor there was a restroom offering privacy enough that she could return to camp without frightening anyone. As she did so, her cell phone rang.

"Hello?"

"Are you outside the building yet?"

"George?"

"Yes."

"Yes, I'm outside the building. Only just," she laughed.

"Good. Then it isn't too early for me to call you. When can I visit you in your part of the country?" he said. Anna laughed again.

∗

George and Anna sat alone at a corner table in a different and nearly empty dining room later that night. She admired the vast view of the three cities which the wall of windows allowedefdx from this height. She could also see from here, the dam in each of those cities, and the water pounding hard behind each.

"So how come a beautiful woman like you went into medicine?"

"And Anthropology."

"And Anthropology."

"It was the numbers of people I saw who couldn't get answers, or even help, from our medical industry. I'm sort of a pattern recognition sort of person."

"Like your mom."

Anna laughed at that. "I sometimes forget that United Sovereignty and my mom are one and the same."

"And that every person in the whole world knows both?"

"Yes. That too."

"You were saying."

"Anyway, medicine at that time figured if they could help a certain percentage of patients - say it was sixty percent maybe - who came in with what they called classic symptoms of something, that was good enough. Among the percentage unable to get answers though, I was able to see patterns - in symptom sets that turned out to be syndromes, and in non-classic presentations."

"And that mattered to you, the remaining percentage?"

"Yes, that mattered," Anna replied, surprised by the question. George paused for a length of time that would have made another uncomfortable, before he spoke again.

"My mom," he began, his voice different now, "was sick a long time before she died. Instead of telling her they didn't know what virus or syndrome or whatever... thing... had her, she heard over and over that nothing had her, that nothing at all was wrong with her. And then she died, after years of struggle on her own without help."

"Arrogant, isn't it?" Anna said quietly, moving her hand over to cover his.

"Very."

They sat like that a moment, then George raised his glass in a toast, moving it toward Anna's. "I'm very glad you decided to go into medicine, Doctor." Anna clinked her glass to his. "As am I, George," she said, "as am I."

*

It was two days later, as Anna was finishing up annual exams for her pediatric patients at her university-based school, that her watch vibrated three times and then three more. She ignored the ringing. Anna didn't bother to have caller ID on her watch. She didn't need it. Anna knew who was calling long before the ringing or the caller ID would have told her.

When the series of three vibrations began again, she finally pushed the button to connect the call. "I'm so sorry," she said to her small patient, continuing with the exam as she spoke. Anna said 'hello' just as she gently placed her scope into the child's ear.

"So, I'm in your part of the country," George's voice said. It wasn't his first call to her since their dinner.

"George?"

"Yours truly." Anna checked the child's other ear.

"Really, you're here?"

"Well, OK, I'll *be* there. Soon."

"Your ears look great," she said to the child, before pausing a moment.

"If you can get here by tomorrow," she added into the phone as if the thought had just come to her, "I can show you my camp." Anna set down her scope and lifted the business end of a stethoscope from her chest. Placing it against the boy's chest, she listened intently.

"You own a camp?"

"Indeed. It seems that I do."

"In that case, I'll be there tonight!"

"Oh!"

"See you tonight!"

"See you...?" Anna began before realizing the line had gone dead.

She returned her full focus to her exam and the boy.

"Sorry. That was... odd," she said with a laugh, but the boy was still staring at the watch.

*

There was a loud buzzing noise as the prison door lock was released and the heavy, metal door slid open to the side. Joe, the security guard Tony had come to know as a friend, walked Tony out into the burning sunlight. Tony reached up and covered his one good eye with his arm.

"It's alright. It'll feel good in a minute," Joe told him. "But then, unfortunately, it'll feel good for *only* a minute more after that." After another couple of minutes, his eye adjusted, Tony was able to lower his arm to soak in the beauty of the warmth and light. His friend was right though, a minute after that and Tony was setting down his paper bag to pull from it his head cover. He tied that on his head and picked up the bag again. Tony turned to the man who'd done so much for him inside.

"You be well, huh. Thanks for everything," he told him. Joe held out his hand to Tony, but they both shared a laugh when Tony grabbed him into a hug instead.

Then Tony turned to look up into the hills and get his first, full, solid view of them. "Walk up hill, huh?" he said.

"That's what they say, my friend," Joe answered. Tony nodded a sharp, quick nod, and then, his cloth on his head and all his worldly possessions in the paper sack in his hand, he started out on his long, long walk.

8

At the ramp leading to the ferry that night, Anna waited in the dusk. Eventually a limousine pulled up to the ramp and George gave a wave. Though thirty feet from where the car had parked, Anna took a single step toward the vehicle and was beside it. George gave a series of blinks as he stepped out from the back of the long car.

Behind them, the ferry pulled up to the dock. George, still bewildered, shook his head again as if to clear it.

"Weren't you just over ...? How did you get...," he said, but Anna just smiled. No less confused than before, George dropped the backpack from his hand to the ground and turned to pull a second pack, like a small duffel, from the limousine.

"I'm glad you could make it," Anna said.

"Yes, yes, me too, I'm so glad it..." but Anna interrupted him with a lengthy kiss. Then, just as suddenly, she leaned over and picked up his backpack from the ground.

"So, shall we roll then?" She turned without waiting for his response and headed for the ferry with his backpack. George, still shaking his head, followed her carrying his bag.

"Roll. Right. We should... do that, we should... roll..." George's voice trailed off as he walked.

The ferry pulled away from the dock and out of sight.

*

It wasn't till the next morning that George found himself at an old-fashioned trail head saddling horses with Anna. A woman he'd never met was also there and she was saddling one of three horses.

"George, this is Gabby. Gabby, George," Anna said.

"Nice to meet you," Gabby said to George, sticking her hand out toward him. He shook it and returned the greeting.

"What is this camp about, Anna?" Gabby then asked.

"Ya, I'd like to know the answer to that too, Anna."

But in answer, Anna laughed.

"What? What is it?" Gabby said, she and George looking at each other to try to understand.

"It's just that, well, you're both of you essentially 'rock stars' and neither of you knows who the other one is," Anna laughed again.

"Not totally true," George puffed, "I know that she's a, like a, scientist, of some sort or ..."

He looked to Gabby, who, pretending for a minute like she might have an idea, jumped in with, "And I know that he's a... I saw him at that one..." but then quickly finished with, "Ya, I got nothing," before all three were laughing.

"The answer to your other question," Anna said after they'd settled down again, "is that you will both see soon enough."

"Well, that clears that right up," George said to Gabby who laughed. The three mounted up.

"Why doesn't your horse have a saddle?" George asked.

"Same reason Shasta wasn't hitched to the post with a lead like your horses, she and I communicate thoroughly well without either."

"Oh, I see. Again, that clears that right up," George joked, causing Gabby to start laughing all over again as the horses walked.

*

The horses had brought them now, to a place where, far in the distance, they could make out more modern buildings.

"All four of the areas here offer well-appointed accommodations, stores, several styles of school. People from all the residences interact daily, but each area has a theme and residents do get to choose the area, or theme, for their living quarters, that best suits them. There is a Gatherer-Hunter area here. Up there is a sort of space-explorer themed area that is more about what most humans think of as the future." Anna continued pointing. "Over there is Transport Hall and up ahead there, is the medical center."

Gabby whistled appreciatively. "Impressive," she said. "You did all of this?"

"Not alone, of course. I had a team to implement the designs. One of my favorite little touches, little hidden details here, is that in each of those two buildings there is a wall with a series of plaques. Those plaques list name after name, of women who, throughout history, have contributed valiantly yet for the most part, unnoticed, by society."

"I am also impressed," George said, "but I need you to go back a minute. What do you mean, 'people *think of* as the future'?"

"If reality actually existed in eleven dimensions, but humans can't comprehend the implications of even four or five, what would a being who thinks in all eleven dimensions seem like to you?" she said.

Anna made a noise then, to break her horse into a run. The noise wasn't for Shasta though, that signal was for her human companions. The others did the same and the three let their horses run hard, galloping through the meadow, letting the horses feel their legs, the wind, the sun. It was short-lived though, as the depleted ozone affected the animals too.

Just outside one of the more modern looking buildings on the 'future' themed side of camp, the three dismounted and walked toward the door of the building.

"These two buildings are complete and self-contained. Able to meet all the needs of the very special kinds of people housed, and educated, inside."

Anna reconsidered her words as she pulled open the door for the others.

"Not educated exactly. It's more bi-directional than that really. We learn from them, they learn from us, all grow in whatever ways each chooses. We each learn from all the others really."

The three walked down a long hallway. George peered into the first open door and saw what appeared to be biological and chemical experiments. He crossed the hall to where Gabby was peering in at another open door. That room also had experimental lab work proceeding, but these were of a mechanical and electrical nature.

"It's so …" George let his voice trail off.

"Thank you, I think?" Anna chuckled. "We have tried to think ahead about everything. The hospital, lab, and schools, each has every tool or convenience for which we could plan.

Gabby opened the door and moved to enter.

"I would like to introduce you a bit later if waiting isn't too big a challenge, Gabby?"

Reluctantly Gabby closed the door again. "If I must," she said.

"Excuse me, Dr. Anna?"

"Ah, Christina." Anna turned to introduce her guests. "Christina has already been here three weeks. She's an apprentice, of sorts. Christina, this is George and Gabby."

"I've heard...! So much... Great things...," she shook Gabby's hand, gushing before her idol like the teen she had so recently been, before turning away to shake hands with George. "Nice to meet you, Sir," was all she said to him.

"Same."

Christina walked with them as they moved into the next wing of the building; the residences. The group passed several rooms as they talked. Gabby noticed that in many of the common areas of the residences, people of various ages were eating or preparing meals or snacks, reading, drawing, playing chess and participating in a variety of activities you'd see just about anywhere.

Anna and Christina showed the guests into an individual residence. This one was empty.

"Gabby, your suite, much like this one, will be ready later today."

"Do *I* get a suite too then?" George asked.

"If you choose to join us you would, your talents are also very valuable to our efforts here – or you'd not have been invited, nor able to access the camp."

George shook his head in disbelief. "You know, for a guy who is never flustered, I find you leave me absolutely speechless far too regularly," George replied.

But Anna had already moved on. Walking at her crisp pace again, she pointed out the classrooms and the wing up ahead. Finally, George jogged to catch up to the group.

At the first classroom, they all stopped. George and Gabby looked in through a window in the door. Children were running and playing and laughing in the room. One girl was reading to herself and her head moved back and forth on the words as fast as the others who ran all around her. She turned pages just as fast.

"At home, all the kids move as slow as the parents, with the heat. Why do these seem to be doing so well in there?" George asked.

"They were born for this, evolved for it. They are an improvement upon us, designed specifically for this climate."

Anna gave them a moment, but her guests were without comment so she kept moving. At the next classroom door, a second group of children was also at work, or play. But when Gabby and George looked through this window, the children's movements seemed at first, incomprehensible.

"These are our Double-Gifteds." Anna explained.

Standing still, arms spread low and eyes closed, the children stood in a circle. Meanwhile, small objects moved slowly around them while other items hovered above them.

"Is that... what it looks like?" Gabby asked incredulously. "Is that group... are they... moving objects without their hands?" She looked at her own hands and back again to the children as she said this.

Anna let the guests watch for a while, soaking in what they were seeing. Then she added another surprise.

"You might be doing that soon too, I told you that you have another gift of which you are yet unaware."

Both guests laughed deeply at that.

"You will," Christina said. At the twin looks of doubt she received, she continued. "When the kids and In-Citiers arrive, they begin their lessons, whenever each is ready, there is no rush. But we learn to focus our mental gifts, and to strengthen them."

"In-Citiers?" George asked.

"Those from the city whose strengths allow them to make it through Athena's Gates," she said. Then she blushed a little. "Well, that's what Hala calls them anyway."

"Doesn't everyone "make it through?" Gabby wondered.

"No. The Out-Citiers can't. They end up living on the other side these days, coming up not knowing they won't be able to enter." Christina said.

"There's no 'us' and 'them,' Christina," Anna gently said. The girl blushed again.

"Does everyone have... mental gifts?" George asked.

"You and Gabby do. Or you wouldn't have been able to make it through the Gates. I'll point those out to you when we walk up the hill," Anna said.

"What's it like so far, Christina? Living here? Being here?" Gabby asked.

"Amazing. Every day here I feel like I'm awake and everyone else is asleep, like I've pulled away but everyone else is still attached to the machine that lulls all of humanity."

The two were still contemplating that when a young girl of nine or ten stopped in front of them. Where she had come from neither George nor Gabby could say, but she smiled at Gabby, took her hand, and led her passed a long row of windows to a door they hadn't yet seen. The others followed Gabby and the girl.

"This is Chantel," Anna explained. "She's been with us more than two years now. Chantel, have you met Delia yet, she arrived just last night."

"Yes. We are having fun together this morning," the girl said without altering her pace.

Chantel stopped for only a moment when she'd arrived at the door, then the door opened and they could see that it exited to the outside and a playground. Chantel walked out and stopped just in front of a jungle gym. Still holding Gabby's hand, she turned and looked up into Gabby's face.

"You're one of us," she told Gabby. Gabby crouched beside the girl so that their faces were on the same level.

"Yes. I am. I didn't know about this place though and had to live out there."

"Was it painful for you?"

"Very much so. It made me very sick." Here, Gabby rubbed her abdomen as if to show her. "So sick, that I am glad you can still tell that I'm one of you."

"I can still tell. Can't change it. I'm glad you're here with us now." Chantel smiled at Gabby then, let her hand drop, and climbed up onto the jungle gym as if nothing unusual had happened. Delia was climbing on the jungle gym too. The girl paused and tossed a curt wave.

"Hi Delia," Anna replied. The other two said the same. Delia, gazing intently, said hello back, but quickly returned her focus to the metal bars.

"Thank you so much for bringing me here," Gabby said quietly when they'd walked away from the children.

"You came. I didn't bring you," Anna said, just as quietly. "But, I thought you might feel at home here. You could feel the tug of Truth back there. Not everyone can. You can feel the strength of wakefulness while others sleep."

"I… think now, that may be true. Either way, I thank you."

Christina said goodbye to them then and walked back through the door from which they had come while the other three walked out into the meadow. As quietly as she had spoken, Anna took George's hand in her own as they walked.

"You didn't look surprised by any of that," Anna said.

"No," George answered, I suppose I'm already realizing that anything and everything could happen here, and that nothing should surprise me."

"So, you feel good about it all, then?"

"I do. But then something tells me you knew that I would, as you knew Gabby would."

"I thought you might." They had now arrived to a point on the mountain which gave them the chance to view more than one hundred and eighty degrees of the valley beyond the mountain. As the three looked out over the vast distance, every inch was covered by the presence of humans. But the presence clumped, in places, into three cities, each with its own outlying areas. One each to the North, East, and South of where they now stood and each with its own overflowing, valiantly struggling dam protecting it.

Several areas within these valleys but beyond the Clock Tower and the Red Alien, Anna could see, were nearly completely covered with water despite the dams. They were covered more now than she had observed even just last week on her visit. From here, when she turned, she could also see the old, familiar, landing strip; a long, narrow track of dirt in a meadow of flowers, an old and now rusting plane resting at the end of it.

"In just over a few weeks now, the covering of the land by melted ice pack will have left only isolated pockets of land, like this one, still above sea level." As one, the group turned in the fourth direction and saw the tiny sliver of city in the valley, which they had seen from the window.

"They tell us the dams will hold, because they have to say that. But they won't. Then, those cities too, will be under water as are so many of our global cities already. The water level rises, a little every day."

"But this spot will be spared," George said.

"Yes. Seventy years ago, a woman, a scientist gifted in code breaking created United Sovereignty and set in motion the paradigm shift leading to global peace," Anna said.

"We all learned of it in elementary school," Christina responded.

"Your mother," George murmured.

"Your mother!" Gabby gasped.

"Twenty years after that and everything had changed. Climate change made it clear that the next global catastrophe wouldn't be political in nature. Having graduated from medical school, I set about to locate this property for my patients. That is when this place was born."

"Fifty years ago? Seventy years ago? But you aren't more than forty years old yourself! Are you? How could you have done these things!" Gabby blurted. Anna laughed.

"Indeed, I am not. I shall live many hundreds of years."

"Shall we all then?" Gabby was still exclaiming as if she had to force words passed a blockage in her tightening throat.

"At that time, this new century was not even fifteen years old. I also realized that some of the children who were my patients, they were referred to back then as 'on the spectrum,' and who were skyrocketing in number, were not disabled as was then thought. They were an evolution.

"An evolution?" George said, in awe after so many bewildering revelations.

"Yes. Autistic children are often cold. Their parents reported to me then, years ago, that when they would get fevers, they would behave, with fever, as other children do 'normally.' Anna continued her walk downhill toward their horses and the others followed.

"When they got hotter, they weren't just comfortable but actually better?"

"From a certain perspective. More accurate would be to say that more areas of their brains kicked in. They behaved with more varied function – when they had fevers. In my school, too, I observed, as you did just now, that they huddled, then and now, around any warm object in the classrooms."

"Such as the heaters," Gabby said.

"Such as the heaters," Anna continued. "They were designed for a hotter world then our world then was, you see; a world that would be arriving in just seventy short years. They were an evolution, preparing a new species, one could say."

"A species that could survive the world that would come," George said.

"The hotter world that was coming," Gabby added. "Unbelievable." She sat down, in the dirt, right where she was. "For seventy years, you have been bringing together the people most likely to survive to a place most likely to still be habitable?"

"Indeed. We will leave for a while, for their safety, but then we will return these children here, to re-populate the earth."

"You will be in danger! When others find this place," George said. Anna laughed.

"It may be that you turn out to enjoy Protector status, George," she laughed again before explaining. "Others will run uphill, yes, when the water comes, you see. But we will be in no danger. There is a type of fence if you will, a filter, surrounding this camp.

Anna started walking again, Gabby and George followed.

"A filter?"

"Sort of. For now, you can think of it that way. You see not all who we call people are at the same level of "evolution," so to speak. There are those who, like yourselves, have never… 'fit in' quite right, you might say. For them, something has always felt just a bit, I don't know, off," Anna finished. Gabby and George, nodding, looked at each other and then back to Anna.

"Yes. That's right. Just a tickle of a feeling at first," George said.

"But then it gets stronger." Gabby said.

"Yes. Just like that," George agreed. Their experience had been the same.

"Indeed," Anna too agreed, having watched the process a thousand times. "Just like that. It is that essentially, which the Gates filter." She paused. "But, it is much bigger than that at the same time."

"Of course, it is," George laughed, drawing out the first syllables.

"Here, let me show you," Anna said.

Anna closed her eyes and George and Gabby stood waiting for her to point at something. In a moment, they looked at each other, then back again to Anna. Gabby was about to ask Anna what they should be looking for when suddenly everything had changed. The scene that had been in front of them was gone.

In its place was something else entirely. Some… material, light and gray, that looked a little like clouds, rain clouds, but thinner, parted in front of Gabby and George.

The part widened and behind it the two saw a scene they could not completely grasp.

People were moving about, proceeding in the business of the day, but now the people appeared to be dressed in garments out of a history lesson and the business of the day appeared suddenly to be commerce. Most confusing was that it was now a city setting… and that city looked a lot like… ancient Greece.

The scene moved then, and instead of being in front of them now, it was as if it were below them and they, flying by just a few feet above it. Yet still, they were, at the same time, also a part of this world Anna was showing them, though neither observer understood how this could be.

They came to meadows beyond the city and there they saw more people dressed oddly - in ancient styles. One of these people was leading a seemingly old horse by a worn tether. Equally worn sandals on the man's feet kicked up a little dust.

The three passed by that as well, continuing toward another region where soldiers in battle gear practiced their arts. Some were yelling loudly for or against those engaged in the various one on one competitions of hand to hand combat and other tests of the skills of soldiers.

They continued moving until before them, they saw the rocky cliffs upon which sat the famous citadel known to every school child. Within The Acropolis, they saw the many buildings including the temple to Athena Parthenos - The Parthenon. Dedicated to the patron saint of Athens, The Parthenon was watched over by an enormous bronze statue of its patron in full battle gear, an equally enormous sword in her hand and uplifted in protection of her city. An owl, also worthy of her in size, rested on her shoulder.

As they got closer to the statue, its face became more visible to them. Closer still and there, before them and cast for the ages in twenty-five-hundred-year-old bronze, stood Anna.

Just as suddenly as the scene had arrived, it was gone and the cloudy gray material was in front of them, before that too was gone and they stood again where they had been, on the ground of the ridge line overlooking the camp.

There was no time to consider what had just happened or even what they had seen because Anna had already started walking. The two jogged to catch up to her.

Anna was still slightly in front of them when they rounded a bend on the hill. They saw their horses not too far from them to their right. Beyond that and further up the hillside, they also saw a crowd of people gathered. The crowd was not gathered in the normal way, but was spread out in a line, the way they would if there were a wall right at that point in the hillside.

"Out-Citiers," Anna said. "Those who come from the cities below who cannot pass through the Gates. And, of course, those are the Gates."

"What? Where? Where are the Gates?" George asked in amazement.

"You can't see the Gates. They're invisible. But, they parted just now, and through them, we traveled. We can open them on any time or place in the universe. Those people who can't get through them, though, can *feel* them. It feels to them just as if it were concrete they were up against."

It was Gabby's turn now, to murmur incoherently to herself. "A worm hole? Through *time,* not space? A *stable* worm hole?" Her muttering continued.

"There are an infinite number of stable wormholes, you just have to open the one you need, the right one. We use them all the time in telepa-porting."

At this, Gabby's mumbled words stopped altogether and she stared in silence.

George however, had put together a different two data points. "So, United Sovereignty," he said, speaking into the sudden void, "was never your mother at all, that was you," he said.

"So, that line of people," Anna said, forcefully re-directing them both, "that circles the camp, it lies just the other side of our Gates." Even as she pointed, some of the Out-Citiers were sitting, others were standing about or walking exactly along that line.

Still others though, appeared to search. One Out-Citier carried, covertly, what looked to be a length of cardboard. He carried this into a small shack of three walls. Still being discreet, the man wove this cardboard into one side, one wall, of the little shanty. While he did this, a dirt covered woman came out from inside the small dwelling and looked up at him.

The previous thoughts of Gabby and George dissipated as the three stood quietly, contemplating the scene, digesting its implications. After some minutes, it was George who broke the stillness.

"My brother, William," he said finally. "He's out there. Somewhere. He's... a Wall Street type. He... I know him... he's not going to make it through, is he?" Anna took George's hand gently in her own again, in answer, and simply held it.

"He might, George. He still might," Gabby said quietly.

"There is always hope for growth," Anna added, her voice equally quiet.

"You can do it. Can you do it?" George asked.

"I cannot make him change, I can only ask him to grow."

"The Gates, they do that, they ask for growth?" he asked, still looking downhill.

Anna nodded.

A moment more and the three turned and headed back. Walking toward the horses they could still see off to their right, Gabby asked what was on both their minds. "What is going to happen to them, to these people, now?"

"We will be forever safe from them, from their fear and violence, now." They walked in silence at that.

"We're going to ride back now, to the other part of the camp," Gabby said. "But, from what you have said, I am thinking the people in all parts of camp are a whole lot the same whether they prefer time periods past, or time periods future."

"Indeed."

"But those people, out there, the… Out-Citiers, they are completely different, in the ways that matter, aren't they" Gabby said.

To that, Anna smiled a restrained little smile that was at the same time, also a calm, sad, beautiful smile.

"I knew your perceptiveness would be vast, Gabby," she said, the same restraint in her voice as in her smile.

"No difference really, I think, in all the people, in all the world, except the ability to see that one truth." This time it was George who'd spoken. The three had reached their mounts and each threw a leg up and over and shifted themselves up onto the horses.

"You on the other hand," Anna said to George, "continue to surprise me. I couldn't have said that better myself." Slowly, the horses walked them away from the post and it seemed the animals were as contemplative as the humans.

9

Anna sat on the couch, sipping tea, in the home of her young friend, Jake. She sat across from Jake's mother and father, both in their mid-thirties, as Jake sat on the floor at his parents' feet, deeply engaged in his interactions with a rather large rag doll.

"Lady came here in worms. Space traveler," Jake told the doll. Like Chantel, Jake too, was nine years old. Like Chantel, he was also double-gifted – both autistic and psychic. He held the doll's mouth up to his ear.

"You have a special son," Anna said.

"Yes," said Jake's mother simply.

Jake stood up then and walked over to where Anna sat.

"You are special lady," he said to Anna, cocking his head as he did so.

"Yes, I am," she stated truthfully, without conceit. Jake stared at Anna a moment or two. Then, he turned to his parents.

"She is good," he announced, directing the statement primarily toward his mother. "I will be safe with her for always." Jake then turned and as if he'd not just made a life-altering pronouncement, sat cross-legged upon the carpet and returned to his interactions with the doll. Anna allowed the parents to sit in silence for a few moments more, digesting all that their son's statement implied.

"Did you know he is double-gifted?" she gently asked.

"*Double*-gifted? No, I don't think we...

"Some people call it psychic, his second gift. What is really going on though is that people with the gift are more attentive with the five senses they do have. They don't have six senses as many think, they simply relate to their senses at a different level than do most others." Anna paused. "You've been to visit the camp. May I ask how you, and he, liked it?"

"Oh, he loved it very much," said Jake's mother.

"It was very nice," said Jake's father. "He felt safe. It offers him opportunity, far beyond anything we..." He paused here, in answering, as his eyes had swollen with tears.

Anna sensed her moment to go and she stood. She set down her tea and reached into her bag for her business cards. Anna gave two to Jake's mom who was now comforting her husband, then she crouched beside Jake and said good-bye.

"Any time you would like," she said to the parents when she stood again, "just say the word, all three of you and any other siblings can come stay at the camp for as long or as little as you all like. Please, be my guest."

"Thank you, that's so... we would love to," the father stumbled some, in his gratitude.

"Thank you. For everything. You've been great," his wife added.

"I'll hope to see you all very soon."

"You will," she said, escorting Anna to their front door as her husband contemplated Anna's card.

Anna had twelve more stops to make that day.

*

Gabby heaved down hard on the rope, sweating in the heat. Outside the building housing her science lab, she was able now to raise the heavy 3D printer above the trolley cart as Christina and Hala walked up.

"What are you doing?"

"Moving... this... printer," Gabby grunted. Christina laughed.

"What I meant was... why are you using a rope?"

"The rope?" Gabby just stared back at Christina, blankly, then looked questioningly at Hala. She had no idea what the younger woman could be talking about.

In answer, Christina smiled at Hala then just closed her eyes and stood there, still smiling. To Gabby's amazement, the rope went slack and the printer lowered, gently and slowly, into place on the cart.

"I... don't..." Gabby sputtered. "I thought... I can't...," was all she finally managed.

"You thought you can't is just about exactly right," laughed Christina.

"I am bio-AI," Hala added. "It might help you to think of your brain as also bio-AI – as a bio-computer of immense capacity."

"See, it's your way of thinking that has to change. Protective thinking, yes, but also isolating, and limiting," Christina said.

Then she and Hala were gone and Gabby was left to stare curiously after them, wanting to be able to do what Christina had done.

*

Inside Transport Hall, a man, just the slightest hint of graying to his hair, entered the room across from where Anna was sitting. It was from this spot that she made her visits to the children and their families.

"You needed something, Doctor?" he asked Anna.

"Yes, Haldor, thank you. George is wandering around. The sense I'm getting from him is a desire to be of more help."

"I see," Haldor said.

"At the same time, Gabby would like to learn all that we can teach her here. So, would you please go find them both. I feel their readiness now, to begin. Escort them to their lessons, if you would."

"Understood." With a brief nod the man departed.

*

Haldor led his two charges down a hallway. At one of four doors labeled, *Lesson Room*, the three stopped. It was the same one, Gabby remembered, that they had passed two days earlier. The three entered this room and George and Gabby immediately recognized Chantel and Delia in a focusing session. Christina was in that group as well, which was rounded out by four other children and young adults.

Spoons, small toys, and several small balls were floating in the space directly above the circle made by Christina and the six other gifted youths. Chantel waved to Gabby then, just as they walked in, and one of the little balls fell to the ground and bounced playfully away.

"Chantel," Christina said with a laugh. Chantel jumped to her feet.

Haldor pointed to an area of the room to the right of the children and said, "Over here, we have the..."

"I'll get it!" Chantel yelled.

"With your mind, Chantel, with your mind," Christina reminded her. Chantel sat down again, crossed her legs and said, "Oh. Ya. Forgot." She focused, eyes closed, with her hands resting loosely on her knees.

Haldor, meanwhile, continued describing the room and its contents to the newcomers. But, as he spoke, the ball stopped where it rolled, then paused briefly before rolling quickly and directly back to Chantel. Happily, she grabbed it up, laughed, and yelled, "I did it! I did it!"

Christina's head snapped around toward Gabby though. Haldor too, stopped mid-sentence, to stare at Gabby.

"What did you...?" Christina sputtered.

"Me?" Gabby looked at George, but Christina seemed to be speaking to her, and not the man beside her. "I did nothing, wasn't it the child?"

Beside Christina then, and just above where Chantel sat in her circle, Haldor and George now saw all the other small objects with which the children had been working. They had been joined by many other small objects from the room until there were at least five dozen objects. All the objects now orbited around each other in a way that formed the constellations of the northwest section of the Spring sky.

"Who *are* you?" Christina asked Gabby. "With whom have you been studying?"

"I have no idea what you are talking about."

Christina and Haldor exchanged looks. Even George now looked at Gabby in a way that combined awe with just a touch of fear.

"I... see," said Christina. She stood and bowed from the hips in Gabby's direction. "Thank you," she said, "for joining us today, Maestra."

"You... are... welcome?" Gabby said.

"Team, Chantel has made significant progress today. We share in your joy, Chantel. Well done." Delia and the rest of the children added their congratulations.

"Why is she acting like that, Haldor?" Gabby asked.

"Well, you see, Doctor, the abilities of all other Empaths here, those are known quantities, including yours, George. It was only the full extent of your own which were, and apparently remain, not yet fully quantified. Therefore, the only Empath who could possibly have done *that*, Miss Gabby, is you." Haldor bowed as Christina had done.

"This way," Haldor added after a moment's reflection, and the three walked again, this time toward a counter. On the counter, they found various candies in colorful bowls.

"These are for focus practice. Normally, we set them on the table, mentally focusing on only one till your focus is so strong that all else falls away and the world consists of only this one thing."

Haldor turned his back to them for a moment as he gathered a few additional items for the work session.

"Obviously, that will be a little different..." Haldor began. He stopped speaking when he turned again toward Gabby and George. There, in the air in front of them hung all the candies; they were suspended so as to render the profile of Dr. Anna. But this time, Gabby was smiling with obvious enjoyment. Haldor was momentarily speechless. Even as he stared, the toys too, returned to their previous constellation positions above the children.

"Well, okay then..." he finally managed.

"This, I think, might be where we part ways into separate work groups, Gabby and I," George said.

"You think?" was all the response Haldor could come up with and George threw back his head and laughed.

*

A half an hour later, George sat at a table in the lesson room, his hands on his thighs, his feet flat on the floor. In front of him on the table were the colorful bowls of gummy-chew candies. Haldor had escorted Gabby to another group and told him to stay here and focus on the candies. He stared so hard at them now, that he was surprised when they didn't burst into flame.

Behind George, the group of children with Chantel, Delia and Christina was still playing. A second group, this one mostly of young adults, had entered while he'd sat there, and it was to this group that Gabby had been added. They appeared to be working on self-levitation. They were working with an older instructor George didn't recognize.

Gabby hadn't recognized her either. She had felt uncomfortable, at first, coming over here with Haldor, being separated from George. Now, she was feeling a little better about it because, she reasoned, how long really would she have been able to make the candies interesting?

A young man beside Gabby lifted off the floor. He floated slowly, easily, around and above, the circle. Haldor had been standing, watching her, from somewhere between her and George, and she had the vaguest notion of him rolling up onto his tiptoes in excitement as she slipped, eyes closed, into the deepest peace she had ever known. And then she, Gabby, floated too. Two inches at first, then a foot, then Gabby floated three feet above the floor. She was aware only that all noise in the room had come to a stop. The sudden silence caused George to turn in his seat.

When Gabby got five feet above the floor, she slowly closed into a ball, grasping her hands in front of her shins.

Slowly, she rotated forward, doing an in-place somersault. She stopped, then reversed direction and did a backward somersault. She floated down to the floor and stood in her spot in the circle again. She opened her eyes and for a long moment, there was stillness in the room before Christina finally spoke.

"You never needed my help with the printer at all, did you?" she said to Gabby. But Gabby, who had been unaware that she hadn't needed help, had no reply.

"I told you that you were one of us," Chantel said. Gabby felt something she'd never experienced before, but which she recognized immediately. Gabby was home.

10

Tony was gone from the prison now. The absence of his leadership had already been felt, and the ramifications of that impact were slowing building. The fear, felt more strongly inside this cage, rippled and grew at the same rate as the white caps behind the dam. Guards, administration, inmates, all were unsure of the next few days and weeks and as such, none were immune to the churning, building consternation within, that comes with uncertainty and imminent danger. That fear could be felt throughout the prison building, bouncing along and intersecting with the leadership void brought about by Tony's recent departure.

Into that void stepped three prisoners with a plan for action. The three entered the cafeteria as one that morning. The whole building and everything in it hummed vividly on that particular morning, with the same curious energy. Would it be four weeks, four days, four hours? Would it be less time than that before the dams would break and their city, their prison, would be underwater like every city before them? The news stations claimed they would hold, but by now, everyone felt that was unlikely. When would it be? How much time did they have? The energy of these questions was palpable in the cafeteria as the inmates – one short man leading two tall – shared furtive, conspiratorial looks between themselves and made their plan into action.

The three knew there would be several large groups of inmates in the cafeteria so when they passed one of these groups and pulled their short, homemade shivs from their socks, it was a random choice of group and had not been pre-determined.

They had agreed ahead of time only that any of the groups would suffice, all they needed was the cover of a great many people – any people. Standing behind this group, they each quickly stabbed a fellow inmate. The cuts were not deep, but they were sufficient. For all that had been needed was chaos. It was the chaos, and not the injuries, that was central to their plan.

Three security guards, seeing the stabbings, ran to the group from different sections of the room. In moments, the chaos had become a brawl. Only seconds after that, the guards were held tight by inmates and the motion shifted as the whole mob moved, as a unit, toward the external doors. The short leader of the original three yelled as they approached the doors.

"Open them doors!" he bellowed.

A disconnected voice answered them through the P.A. system. "Walk away. A dozen guards are on their way to the cafeteria as we speak."

"Shit," yelled the short leader at the voice, "you don't got no dozen guards no more. They done run from this water. Let us run too. We only want what's fair, but 'less you open them doors right now, you gonna have three dead guards on your hands."

There was a few seconds of silence, as if the ethereal voice was thinking this over, before they all heard the loud buzzing noise, plain as day, that signified the unlocking of an exterior door. This noise today though, was multiples louder than that, and it took a moment more for those gathered to realize just why. Not this one door, but every door in the prison – in the cells, in the activity rooms, in security bays, all of them – had been opened all at once. The buzzing could have been deafening if it weren't for the noise of the free-for-all as the inmates moved toward freedom the way a river moves toward the ocean – without a care for any other thing that might lie in its way.

From the outside of the building, it looked like an orange explosion, a dangerous elementary school letting out for recess. Each reacted to the sunlight as he passed into it, but did so without stopping or slowing, as each ran in a direction as fast and as far from this building, and hopefully, the coming water, as they could.

Inside the prison, in the small booth of a room toward the back, which served as security HQ, only the monitors on the counter, the PA system, and a few overturned chairs could be seen. That room, like the rest of the prison, was suddenly devoid of life. The many monitors showed regions of the prison both near and far. The scenes on most rotated a shift of four locations. But not one of those rotating scenes showed life either. There was only the one shot that showed any change at all and it was on a separate, non-rotating monitor held solidly on a view of the rear doors.

That shot showed double doors bursting outward, and six guards and their supervisor hurtling through them. The seven men, like the prisoners before them, reacted to the sun, doing so without stopping or slowing, while moving off, each man in a direction of his own choosing. Each moved as far from the water, the inmates and each other as he could get.

11

Gabby floated freely outside of the restraints of the earth's atmosphere. George too, floated loose near her side, a sense of wind pushing and pulling at his clothing.

"We have been," Anna said, and the two heard her clearly inside of themselves though Anna herself was not close, "for decades, focusing and strengthening the abilities of those here, to recognize and store their own patterns and transport themselves, or telepa-port." It was Anna's strength of mind, and not yet their own, that held Gabby and George where they were. "Focus now, yourselves, on your oneness with all people, now and who have ever been born. That connectedness will show you, will open for you, the pathways between people. That is where you will find the pathway to here, and beyond here. That is where is stored the knowledge for holding your patterns, for finding worm holes, and for telepa-porting."

Neither Gabby nor George fully understood what they had felt being spoken inside them, but, trusting Anna, they both focused hard on the ideas anyway as they spun slowly in space, floating as though swimming. How long Anna held them there, allowing them this experience they couldn't yet allow themselves, neither of them knew. But it was as George was tiring, and feeling the fatigue of the journey, that Gabby suddenly was gone from beside him. He felt Anna speak inside him again.

"That path of connection can be traveled on, through time and space," her voice said. Was she speaking to Gabby then? George wondered.

"There's the wormhole!" Gabby said, but still George could not see her anywhere. George felt himself being suddenly moved then. He gained immense speed and traveled rapidly through space until he slowed again and landed, gently, on the Space Station Anna had intended as their destination. A grouping of signs, in what appeared to be different languages, danced across monitors above him. The one in English referred to where he now was as simply, The Station. Gabby reappeared suddenly, beside him.

"Where did you go?"

"It was amazing, George. I was focusing like Anna told us to, on the destination that was in my mind, when a pathway appeared in front of me. I was able to travel here on it!"

"Without Anna's help?"

"For that short stretch of the trip, yes. I was alone, moving under my own power."

"Huh. I'm not so sure that's something I'll ever be able to do."

"You will," Gabby said, simply. "It was like transporting and the wormhole were the *same* thing though, George, and not two different things at all." She might have said more but it was then they realized they were standing among creatures from throughout the universe. They spoke no more while they looked around, trying to take in the sheer vastness of the differentiation they saw.

An enormous number of species moved, some quickly, some slowly, in what appeared to be a lobby-type area of a large transportation depot. Vehicles of some sort were stopping to let on or let off, a multitude of passengers. George saw another sign, this one indicated they were at International

Station Organization Number V1.0651. Below the station number was a list of times and, he could only imagine, places.

A creature ran up to them as they gawked about them. It came only to their lower shins and was covered in fur that stood up on end. It reminded Gabby of a creature with its finger in an electrical outlet. The fur was completely round and if it had feet, they were unseen beneath so much fur. The effect was as though a ball of pointy fur were floating quickly toward them. They could see two dark, little, gumdrop eyes as the creature got closer. The creature yipped at Gabby's feet and then ran off. Then they noticed that creatures like these but in many shapes and sizes, were intermittently about the depot. They seemed to always accompany one or another of these other beings. Almost immediately, another of the creatures had run up to them. This one was taller and with more visible legs.

"I'm sorry!" they heard a voice yell to them. A being, seemingly male, was standing beside several large crates, waving madly toward the creature.

"Like my yellow lab pup when I was a kid!" Gabby said, bending to pet the sweet thing. As she did so she was overcome by the desire to take a deep, deep breath.

"Weird," she said to George when she had done so, "but I can breathe better. I feel... happier."

George bent and took a deep breath too.

"Wow," he said.

The two repeated the action several more times. The being that had been yelling after the creature finally stepped away from his crates and made it through the crowd, stopping alongside Gabby. She stood just as the being bent to pet the creature that had reminded her of her long-ago puppy.

"I hope he wasn't bothering you," his voice came through a metallic device before the sounds reached their ears.

"Not at all, we enjoyed petting him," George said.

"But," Gabby started, not knowing really, what else to say. "I think, that he, maybe, helped us to breathe better. Is… is that crazy?"

"Oh, oxygen breathers! You must be new here. Happy to know you, Antares is the name! L'Arbradogs!" he said. But the two could think of no suitable reply to such a thing, so the man continued. "You know, pets? Well, an experiment, originally. Quite successful. To cross an arbor of trees with an Earth pet. They breathe in CO2, and breathe out…"

"Oxygen?" George interrupted him.

"Quite right. Tweeking the bio-engineering took forever, but they're good now. They will return to earth with many other species, some years from now. We've not had too many visitors from that planet yet. This device allows all of us, from anywhere, to communicate between languages though."

Behind them an announcement in a language that was not English was heard.

"Well, that's us, gotta get my cargo loaded. Sure hope my little guy wasn't a bother."

"Oh no, not at all, very cute!" Gabby said. The man nodded, and his pet by his side, they headed for the vehicle loading platform.

George and Gabby became translucent a moment later. Then, they both, at the same time, disappeared.

*

Back on Earth, both re-appeared in front of Anna. Anna waited to speak until they had completed the process.

"So, you see, you will need to help in your transport, I can hold you there on my own, only so long."

"You must teach me to do that better," Gabby said.

"Not you, George?"

"I don't see me doing anything like that any time soon. Gabby is already far further along in the process than I am, I'm afraid."

"It is true, some begin with greater gifts, with less debris, but all who hold the seed of possibility inside them will, in time, arrive."

*

That evening, Anna sat peacefully, quietly, in a favored spot along the hillside above camp. The beauty, and relative cool, of the setting sun, and the sounds of the crickets and the camp, surrounded her. From here, in one direction, all the valleys, and the water threatening them, were visible. In the other, the outline of the full moon was now, in the reduced atmosphere, as visible as the ridge line beneath it.

George approached on foot and stayed respectfully back. "I don't mean to intrude," he said to her.

"I felt your approach. It's alright, George. Come, sit, it's no intrusion to be cared about." George sat in the soft grass beside her. It was lovely here, he realized.

"This is a beautiful spot."

"Isn't it though? There was a wonderful character. Long ago. Pooh Bear he was called. He had his Thoughtful Spot. I have mine."

"I like your, *Thoughtful Spot*, is it? I can see why you chose this one." Together, they sat in silence a long, pleasant time.

"I imagine I know what it is that's got you thoughtful."

"Oh?"

"Those families that are still out there…"

"We can't leave them out there."

"I know. I can smell the desperation out there, when I go out near the Gates. I wish there were a way to get them all here, all at once. But, with things the way…"

"There is, actually. It's that I've been thinking about," Anna interrupted.

"There is?"

"Yes. *I* could do it. I could get them all here."

"You… could do it? By yourself?"

"Yes. I've just… never brought that many before."

"What will happen?"

"Not totally sure. I'll be vulnerable afterwards, that much I know. The camp too. For a day or two I won't be able to coalesce the protection of the camp."

"Do you protect it now?"

"Not alone. All the minds here contribute. I coalesce the protection though, and form it into a unified solid. If we leave nearly as we arrive though, it might not matter."

"You mean telepa-porting everyone away from here? To the station out there?"

Anna nodded.

"While you are bringing everyone in? And holding the Gates together?" he asked, incredulous. Anna looked at him, but said nothing in reply.

"Will such an attempt injure you?" George asked, "will you be harmed?" Again, she looked but said nothing. "Why won't you answer me? You! You…" He stopped, understanding hitting him full in the face.

"No!" he said. "You can't do it, absolutely not, it's too much to ask of you, it isn't fair!"

"See," Anna laughed, "Protector Status. It's your truest nature." But, neither that nor his awareness that the fear that had hold of him, was almost childish in nature, did anything to mollify or appease this feeling he'd never known before.

"Walk with me?" Anna asked, standing. George stood too and the two walked along the ridge line together. He took her hand in his, though that required a boldness beyond what that simple act had ever required of him before, with other women.

They neared the Classroom Building. Here, lingering near the building, the moon behind them, George stopped Anna for a moment and her momentum spun her toward him.

"I don't want you to try something that could kill you," he said plainly. Anna was surprised.

"It's not often I'm surprised, George, but this isn't about you or what you want, or me, or..." But Anna's words were stopped by George's kiss. He kissed her by the light of the full moon. She kissed him back with the knowledge of a thousand millennia before them and a thousand millennia after them coursing through her.

"Our first kiss," he said, smiling down at her.

"Second, actually."

"Ah, but we *both* participated in this one," he laughed, "so, I'm counting this as the first real one," he said and she smiled.

"You know I have to do this, George," she said after a long moment.

"Yes," he said, "I do. I know."

12

The next morning, just as the sun broke the horizon, George and Anna entered Transport Hall together. A large, open room with an oversized throne-like chair at one end, this room was not one George had yet been to see.

Six of Anna's Protector Status residents were already there, awaiting her.

"Will they stay with you?" George asked.

"They will. They are to protect the children arriving while I cannot."

"I would like to stay as well." At that, she stopped walking. She looked at him.

"I would like that too."

"But, I cannot?"

"One day, perhaps."

"I thought as much. I will do what I can to help from outside then, if I must."

"Thank you, George."

He wanted to say more, but there was nothing more to say. He forced a smile and exited the room, leaving Anna to her work. Anna continued to walk. She looked at each of the six Protectors, then to the last one, she nodded.

Then Anna sat down in the large, flat, un-cushioned chair. She stilled herself.

She placed one palm flat on each arm of the chair.

She gathered herself, and focused.

Then, she began to vibrate. It was a movement below the range of visible frequencies, it matched that of a specific wave, felt only in deepest space.

A moment later, Anna moved through space. At speeds of four million miles a minute, she could hurtle through time and through space. Today such speeds wouldn't be needed, she was staying within Earth's atmosphere today.

It took only a moment before she saw in front of her, the specific small, suburban house she sought. Anna slowed herself and entered the home.

Inside the house, there was a child. Anna knew her to be six years old and the child sat on the carpet and played while her mother read the New York Times on the couch behind her. The television was on.

Anna heard the voice on the television, the host of one show or another, speaking as she watched the child play.

"… it was thought that autism was a disability and its increase was not understood. Today we know this to be an evolutionary leap, our knowledge of the extent of their skills expands monthly yet the violence and, some say, jealousy, against them, has never been more prevalent..."

As the voice went on, the child began, subtly, to vibrate. The frequency of her vibration matched that of Anna's. The child stopped her play. Then, she stood. She smiled beautifully and turned to her mother.

"It's time, Mommy," she told her mother.

"Time? Time for…?"

Behind them, unnoticed, the U.S. President and Senate Majority Leader railed on about the violence and what they would do about it.

"It's my time." She hung on playfully to the vowel sound in time, then the girl began to lift from the floor, and become translucent. "I will come for you, Mommy," she said.

Her mother, finally comprehending, stood quickly, knocking the New York Times to the floor.

"Oh! Oh! Already?" she called. But her child was already being transported from the room as they had previously planned.

"Be well!" she called out to her daughter, running to the window. "Be safe! I love you!" And then, to herself, "You are safe now, safe. I will be with you soon."

*

In Transport Hall, Anna reappeared in the chair, as peaceful and still as before she had traveled. In front of her, the translucent child appeared. Through rapid stages, the child became solid before her.

A young Helper Classer approached with a robe. Though she was still clothed, he wrapped it around the girl anyway, to warm her. Then he escorted their newest guest from Transport Hall.

*

Moments later, in a flat in Venice, the process repeated itself. This time the child, who began subtly vibrating before also smiling and standing, was twelve years old. Speaking his mother tongue, he spoke reassuringly to his parents before his departure.

"It is my time," he said. "You will come soon." Then the boy was transported according to plan.

"Be safe, my son!" the boy's father called to him, just before he could see his son no more.

Near a ranch house in the opens of Brazilian cattle country, the process was repeated. The girl was fifteen years old this time and she was riding her horse beside her father on his own mount, across the vast acres of their open ranch land. When the barely perceptible vibration overtook her body, she looked skyward, and then, she too smiled.

"Good bye, Papa," she said in Portuguese. "We will be together again soon!" and then, she too, was transported.

"I love you!" He called out. "I will see you soon!"

In Transport Hall, Anna returned. Again, and again, she returned. The twelve-year-old boy was becoming solid in front of her. The Brazilian girl appeared and slowly, she too, transformed from the glowing, chilled, translucence of travel, to a less ethereal solid.

Anna's next visit was to a cinder block apartment building in Chechnya. This time, Satya, the child to be brought in, was only four. Like all the others, Satya too, felt her body begin a faintly perceptible vibration overtake her. It was there however, that similarities ended.

Instead of being transported by Anna, Satya lifted from the floor, peacefully, slowly, controlled. She moved slowly, in the air, toward her door. Her body began to quietly glow. It became translucent as she moved slowly through the air of her living room.

"I love you, Satya," her mother had time to tell her, in a normal, unhurried voice as the door slowly opened. They hugged before Satya moved passed the open door in full control of her travel. The door closed again, gently, behind her. Satya continued to move through air, through space, under control, to a point mid-way between her home and the camp.

There, at that mid-way point, she met up with Anna, whom she had long been familiar with. Together, the two moved through space, back toward camp and into Transport Hall.

As before, Satya appeared, translucent, in front of Anna, who was herself reappearing in the chair. Satya appeared again as the solid being she was, and Hakon entered with the robe for her. This time, however, Anna waved him gently to the side.

"What happened out there, sweetheart, do you know?"

"I got your message," the girl said. Hakon wrapped the robe around her and she began playing with a small, soft toy left behind in one of the pockets. "You told me about the patterns. You said it was my time to come here. So, I came. I did the thing you said, with the patterns. It was fun."

Hakon cinched the belt of the robe and looked at Anna. She nodded and he walked the girl from the room.

Anna, still standing in the hall alone, reflected thoughtfully. Then she closed her eyes and reached out to The Council.

In five dozen galaxies scattered throughout the universe, the members of her ancient species heard her. For the five dozen of her species who, in their role as protectors of galaxies, made up the Intergalactic Council, their connection happened as though they were all gathered in a single room.

Anna spoke without need of words, to a group of beings without need of bodies. The council members appeared to those of their galaxies therefore, in any, and many, forms and under many names. They appeared to have the ability to shape-shift, though indeed, they had no need of *shape* at all.

"Was it one of you? Did you come?" She asked.

The two, who when they'd visited Earth had been called Nerivik and Torngasoak communicated to Anna that it had not been them who had visited this time. Baubo and Comus, communicated the same.

"Come on, that was a perfect set up, where's your sarcasm, Comus?" Baubo teased him.

"Sorry, that is Momus' department, N'drina" Comus replied, using the term that, in a species that did not comprehend gender, was most close in meaning to sibling. At the same time, it also meant, Dearest One. Variations of the word also acted as the only real name they used for each other; N'dia, N'driri, N'dirga, each of them one by one, was so called.

Their joviality and laughter continued. But then Comus teased Anna, referring to her by several of the dozens of names of Gods and Goddesses with which she had been bestowed through time by various earthlings and their societies – Athena, Christ, Allah, Yahweh, Buddha, Thor, Odin, Ra, Zeus – there had been so many. He never failed to find new joy in this human trait, or in teasing Anna with it.

"It *is* shocking," Nerivik said, "that one from your galaxy understood the message you gave." Anna was pleased to have her topic re-addressed. "We have sent them so *many* creation myths, over time, in an effort to explain. Each time they interpret these explanations by adding conflict, violence, scarcity. It's as if they can't even allow their *stories,* their *imaginations,* to posit peace. What do they want from us already?" Nerivik asked her relative from across the universe.

"Perhaps you really should have chosen a galaxy with a slightly more evolved population to protect, N'drina," Baubo added. "Failing the messaged creation myths, we then, also left the message, a gift, written into their own DNA, in the unused media that is ninety five percent of that DNA. All these means, together we have tried, yet nothing. Still they war. Still they wrongly believe war, violence, to be sewn into the very fabric of their condition."

Anna too, had tried. It was the unused percentage of the average brain of her chosen species that she networked into; in parallel with many, in series with the rest. Through this method, she created the greatest network of bio-computer power in this region of the galaxy.

Each time, she had left behind a feeling, a sensation, a message – a gift for them of knowledge, and of wisdom – inside each brain. Almost all had been ignored.

"After all that, still we tried one last time and we sent them The Messengers. Did they listen then? No, not only did they not listen, they attacked."

"That really is a frightfully unevolved Frankenstein's monster," Torngasoak chimed in.

"A species needs to evolve passed being a danger to the rest of the universe, before connection can be allowed. You know this. You know we never expected *any* of those in your galaxy to do so. That *one* understood our message, that one could understand the pattern coding involved in transporting herself, is better than we could have hoped," Comus said, all sign of jocularity gone as he offered comfort to his fellow protector.

"Is this *one*, though?" Anna asked, insistent. "One born? On Earth, born, one of *us, of our* species?

"I remind you now, only of what you already know, that you cannot save them all. We have all been shown that which might be called prophecy. You seek to save a single planet when you know *we* collectively, must protect thousands."

"But she *is* of us, Satya is, born of Earth, but of the ancient species. A human *has* evolved. She is our species," Anna said.

"Too little, Dear, and much, much too late," came the quiet but honest, collective reply. It was an answer Anna had not wanted, yet had known.

13

Just a few hours later, Anna, on horseback, rode slowly along the camp's perimeter, just inside the Gates. Through the years, many of her chosen species, had come so close to understanding. There had been those who understood transporting, though they believed only mechanical brains could perform the act.

Fifty years ago, in the early 2020s, Anna's hopes for her species had risen again, when a movie had come out. Called, *The Ancients*, it correctly discussed what its writers had called, the Frankenstein Hypothesis. It was that which Torngasoak had referenced. Nothing much had come of it though, to Anna's disappointment. The writers never learned how right they were regarding their premise that humans *had* been visited by her species and by species from other galaxies, but that they'd had to stay unknown; not because they presented any danger, but because humans did.

Humans - for her, her chosen - represented, at their present level of development, a significant danger to the rest of the universe. Anna was saddened by the reality that she would have to leave so many behind. They truly had a seeming inability, or was it an unwillingness, to evolve much at all. Satya though, had been a ray of sunshine for her. One step further than George and Gabby, Christina and all the rest.

Anna and Shasta came upon George, walking on foot along the ridge, as she had known she would.

"Hey," she said quietly.

"Hey," he said. Anna stopped Shasta beside him and he rubbed the horse's neck tenderly. "You're alive." George smiled wanly. "Kind of early for you to be done in the hall already though, isn't it?"

"Things stopped abruptly. A surprise change, really. But, what are you doing down here?" Anna asked him, though she already knew the answer.

"Not sure exactly. Looking for my brother, I guess. Don't talk to him but once a year if that, but somehow..."

"Yes, I know." Anna dismounted. She and Shasta walked along beside George. "I brought you some news."

"Ya? Good, I hope?"

"Good and bad depend on one's perspective, but I'm hoping you'll find this news positive."

"Shoot."

"It came from a little girl. I was bringing her in like all the others, when, just like that, she was bringing herself in."

"*She* did it?"

"She helped do it. Our minds worked on the same effort together. I finished almost as strong as when I'd started."

A loud noised assaulted them just then, from George's left – beside the Gates. They both turned just in time to see two filthy men in rags rubbing their heads and sitting on the ground. The two looked like clones of each other.

"The Gates," Anna said. "Those two couldn't get through." Behind those two men, George saw many others, also dirty, walking up the mountain.

"Are they all coming from the city below?"

"From the cit*ies* below, yes, Distoria, Malanthron, and Antesapiana are all threatened," Anna said. Other Out-Citiers walked along the perimeter, already stuck behind the Gates. All the Citiers were covered in grimy sweat from the excessive heat. George now realized that a few shanties had also been built up, lower down on the hillside. He bent down, crouching, and picked a flower that was at his feet. He held it in his hand and twirled its stem in his hand. Is this, he wondered, what those Citiers who couldn't get through do when they realized they could not go any further?

The shanties seemed to be grouped, very loosely, into two groupings. Each loose grouping had what appeared to be a small cook fire at its center.

"Is that...?" George began. His attention was pulled away by the sight of the two look-alike men now walking toward one of the groupings of shelters. Each man banged together large metal objects as he walked. It appeared they were attempting to frighten the people within that clump of homes. George could not quite make out what the metal objects were that each man held in his grime-covered hands.

"Have factions already...?" A second time, George felt unable to finish his sentence.

"Yes, I'm afraid alliances and factions are a standard fall back for brains of this capacity; An "us," "them" sort of thinking. If they had the capacity to rise above that sort of mentality, to be above attempting to frighten those of what they see as "the other" group, then they'd have likely made it through the Gates."

One of the men turned then and ran directly at George and Anna who still stood behind the Gates. Anna, knowing that the Gates were between them and this man, did not react. George, however, did.

The man hit and bounced off the Gates just as George, still crouched, stumbled quickly backward, away from him, and lost his balance. Both men hit the ground at the same moment. George's flower fell from his hand as he landed in a seated position.

"This," Anna said, "is Xeron. That, over there, is his twin Xenon."

"They…they've attempted to get through before? They already *know* they're going to bounce off?"

"Instead of working to improve what is inside, some prefer to rely solely on force. Over and over, hoping one day, force alone, will be enough."

Xenon now, as if proving the point, ran up behind his brother and, without slowing at all, hit the Gates full force. Xenon bounced off and fell backward to the ground beside his brother. Both sat in the dirt, rubbing their heads again.

"Let Xeron in!" Xeron bellowed at Anna. Xenon however, glared at his brother.

"Let *us* in, don't you mean?!" Xenon said.

Two men ran up from the other shanty village as the brothers quarreled. They carried weapons with them and charged at Xeron and Xenon, interrupting their heated discussion. Anna recognized the two men from the elevator of the financial building she visited for her frequent bank withdrawals in the city.

"These are men from the financial district, George. Perhaps they know your brother, William?"

"*We* will be the group that is given entrance! Not you!" yelled one of the men. Xeron and Xenon also pulled out weapons that, until now, had been hidden within their clothing, clothing that was rapidly turning into rags on their bodies.

The four men engaged immediately in combat and the combat quickly turned bloody. George, saddened, turned away from the battle.

He walked again, this time in toward the camp and no longer along the perimeter. This debacle of humanity was something he no longer cared to witness. But other Out-Citiers were running up to join the battle.

Anna too, turned away. "A decision between a bad option, and a good option, takes no wisdom," she said. "It's the choices between two options that both appear good, which require the discernment of wisdom."

"Are you meaning the safety of those in the camp versus he safety of everyone else?"

"Yes."

"So, you knew what I was thinking then."

"Yes. You were wondering about why we can't just let everyone in. But, if we shifted the rules, let in even one who can't get in on their own, I put at risk trillions of beings."

"Look at them," George said. "What is left out there to be saved anyway?" he mused sadly.

Anna caught up to George and they walked the rest of the way into camp together.

*

Just hours after that, on the same afternoon, when Anna had returned to camp, Jake and his father left their home. They headed for the playground with his favorite truck. Jake's father found a seat on a bench in the shade, and with his son playing in the sand nearby, opened his book.

Jake pretended he was building a great city in the sand. Then he rolled his truck over it and smoothed the sand again. Bored, he moved to the swings and kicked back and forth for a while. He couldn't make it go very well so after a while, he moved on again. He climbed the metal jungle gym instead and hung, upside down, above the sand. His father's bench was now very far away from him.

But it was the odd older boy, and not his father, that Jake was aware of as he hung like that from the apparatus. The older boy was sitting behind where Jake swung from his knees, and was staring intently in his direction. As Jake watched, the boy stood and paced rapidly in front of the small table. He seemed to speak to himself angrily.

Jake grabbed the upper arms of the jungle gym bar from which he hung. He lifted his legs up over the bar and let himself down, lowering himself to the ground and to his feet. He walked over to the boy. Jake stood then, just in front him.

At first, the unknown boy just stared back the way he had been doing from across the playground. Finally, after Jake looked into his eyes for an eternity, the older boy spoke.

"What'd you want?" he barked out at Jake.

"You are filled inside with anger," Jake stated blandly.

"Says who?"

"My name is Jake." Jake's father looked up now, from his book. He watched what was taking place, but of course, on his bench he was much too far away to hear what was being exchanged. He stood and moved toward his son.

"What makes you say so?"

"I can feel things other people..." But here the boy interrupted Jake by pulling a switchblade from out of a pocket. At the same time, he began to shout, loudly.

"I don't say so! *I* don't say so!" he yelled at Jake, and his arms flailed about as he paced. "I'm not bad! I'm not angry, but everyone says that to me, everyone thinks bad about me!"

"You will kill me. The world will change right after, because of it. That which was future, will become present."

The older boy still flailed, still paced. But when Jake's words had finished, the boy stopped moving. He turned, faced Jake and stood still a moment, but only a moment. Then, in a single swift motion, he pivoted closer and buried the blade into Jake's upper chest.

Jake's father's book flew from his hands to the ground as his walking became running.

The boy removed the blade, turned and sank it this time into Jake's abdomen. Then he returned to his pacing, his flailing and his ranting as if he had been uninterrupted, as if nothing much had changed.

"But I'M NOT BAD!" he was yelling.

"Not at all, but your anger makes your actions so," Jake, trance-like, told the boy from where he lay in the sand of the playground. His father reached his side and fell to his knees beside his son. "Let the anger go," Jake said to the older boy, "and it will all be all right." Then a glassy stare took hold of Jake's eyes.

"What?! What the *hell* are you talking about?!" the older boy screamed in demand. Then the older boy ran off toward a clump of houses across the park. Jake's father applied pressure to his son's chest and looked after the boy, wanting to run after him but knowing he wouldn't. Instead he frantically applied pressure to one wound and then the other while he desperately tried to also dial 911 on his mobile.

"Please, come quick. My son, he's been stabbed," he heard himself tell the dispatcher, incredulously. There was already *so much blood*. "We're at a playground. Parfet

Park, in Sunnyside neighborhood, he's badly injured, please hurry!"

Hundreds of miles away, in a different state, and across the country, Anna saw, as though looking through a human-sized crystal ball, the boy running away and little Jake and his father in the now bloody sand.

*

Word of the assault immediately circled the globe.

At the camp, Anna Messaged Hala and Haldor. They were by her side in an instant.

She Messaged the change to them and both implicitly understood – things would now move very fast. There would be next to no time even to mourn the poor boy.

The increasing terror with which those who remained now lived, under the constant threat of the heat and of the water, turned overnight from growing to absolute.

Gabby, moving fast, arrived then, followed quickly by George. Out of breath, she tried to speak.

"Is it true?" George asked for them both.

"I'm afraid that it is."

"That poor boy," Gabby wheezed.

"I will bring the boy's parents here immediately."

"Jake's siblings too, then?" Hala asked.

"He had none."

"After that, will we finish bringing in all the rest?" Haldor asked.

"Indeed. Immediately. We must move fast now, get everyone here. The departure must begin directly after that. The terror is fever pitch now. The prophecy has been fulfilled. The flood, then, is imminent. We can delay no longer."

14

The cement of the dam protecting Distoria, though pummeled by an assault of water with force behind it in the tons, held anyway. Those at the camp, in the city, and in the city's government, watched the dam closely for signs of weakening in the cement. Each day, each hour, that it held, both gladdened and surprised the observers. Today, it no longer mattered. Today was the day and this, the hour, that the water level rose, and the liquid breeched the top of the protective barrier anyway. Today, for Distoria, was the beginning of the end.

A tiny sliver of what would soon become a stream, leaked, drop by drop, down the brief hill into the yards and basements of the closest homes: drops which, on their own and alone, could never threaten a single child, let alone the population of an entire planet.

*

In the closest yard to the dam, two small children played.

"It's time! It's time," one of the children yelled to the other. The families in all the houses throughout the city had been preparing for this moment. Each had prepared an escape plan, suitcases packed and at the ready. Each had trained themselves and their children in what to watch for and above all, to be always observant. The second child ran toward the house, his little sister jumped from the swing she'd been pumping, and ran behind him into the house.

"We gotta go!" her older brother yelled out to his parents as he crossed the threshold into the back of their home.

*

In another yard, a father played at a tea party with his small daughter. Seeing the same breech, the same drops of water that the children had seen in the other yard, he grabbed his surprised daughter quickly from her chair and jumped up from the table, knocking it over with his knees as he did so. Carrying his little girl like a football, he ran for the house. Inside the house, there were bags packed and waiting near the front door.

"The dam's been breeched!" the father yelled to the mother inside.

"Time to go?"

"Time to go!"

She set down the spoon with which she'd been feeding the baby, grabbed the baby from the colorful high chair and walked to the bags at the front. She got there just as her husband did and each put on a large backpack, the father first helping their daughter to put on her much, much smaller backpack. The mother put the baby in a front pack and took her daughter's hand as her husband picked up a large suitcase. The three exited their home for the last time, through their front door, leaving it open behind them.

A few hours later, in the heart of Distoria, the feet of the red alien statue would sit hidden, the alien covered up to the shins in brackish, muddy water.

*

The next morning the hour had come for the same scene to repeat itself with eery similarity at the top of the barrier that protected the neighboring city of Malanthron. The structure held, but the water breeched it anyway.

Drop by drop, and quickly escalating, the water leaked into Malanthron. The residents had seen it all on their news channels before, in cities around the world. As the earth's temperature climbed, water, dripping at first, but soon festooning into wanton streams and wayward rivers, poured through homes, roadbeds, cities, until finally growing into lakes where once a population had thrived. Inside and outside these homes, people observed the water, and flew into uncertain action.

In front of one of the closest homes to this dam, a minivan, loaded with belongings and people, pulled out of its owners' driveway at high speed. The minivan nearly hit a family which was walking in the street behind them. The minivan then overcorrected, moved forward at a crippling angle, backed again with a metallic shriek, and with tires screeching, drove off lurching at high speed, careening all over the narrow suburban road.

As the minivan flew recklessly down the street, broken windows and doors could already be seen in the homes it passed. The looting had begun.

Throughout the neighborhood and the city, fires could be seen and the occasional burst hydrant spewed water from a now additional source, over everyone and their feeble, indeterminate actions. Malanthron's Clock Tower held strong against the rising puddle at its base, and in the distance, Distoria and the Alien could be seen by those fleeing. The drops had become small streams, and these now raced each other down the hill.

*

Later that day, the dam protecting Antesapiana fared the same. The water leaked into the homes, yards, lives and basements of the hardy people of Antesapiana. Everywhere, the water was witnessed as it innocently threatened.

In high rises throughout the city, both those who had been at work and those who had been at home, entered the hallways in droves, pouring in as though humanity too, was a liquid. The workers and homebodies jammed the elevators. People with backpacks and suitcases milled about hallways, unsure what to do now that work was suspended for the day and their ready bags had been located. Others darted about in the hallways, moving frantically without direction. Many paced, others argued, several did both. All tried to decide what was to be done next. Where were they to go now? Chaos was everywhere, worse in the tallest buildings.

In the very tallest of the buildings in Antesapiana, a woman wearing hiking boots and a backpack headed for the stairs instead of the elevator. But, seeing her, others too soon flocked that way. William, still wearing the expensive suit of his work day, was among those who'd seen and then followed the woman. He now carried a backpack just like so many others. On the stairs, he pushed passed a slow moving elderly couple on the stairway and knocked the woman of the couple to the stairs. Her husband, yelling after William, bent to help her, but William just ran on.

In the building's lobby, William then also passed a young mother whose child had gotten injured in the tumult. Though both the mother and the child's bleeding leg were clearly visible, William stepped blindly on the protruding leg as he hurried passed them toward the exit. Behind him, he heard the boy cry out and his mother soothe him while the slow, chaotic, pushing flow of humanity continued to descend.

William tumbled out onto the street, where his ears were suddenly assaulted by sirens, yelling, car accidents, and by trees and walls being knocked over. He also heard random screaming and arguing in all directions around him.

Deval and Patrice, who had been introduced to Anna on the same day as William, sat eating at a sidewalk coffee house. Farther from the dam, those around them were only now being alerted to the coming calamity. The two stood quickly, as one, and Patrice reached down and slipped into her backpack.

"Grab your backpack, Deval. Let's go, we've got to get out of here," she said. Deval reached down and did the same, slipping his straps over first one shoulder and then the other.

"Where? Where are we going, though?"

"No idea!"

The two nodded at each other and walked anyway. But at the other end of the same sidewalk café, they saw a gray-haired woman, sitting alone. She looked dazed, uncertain. The two kids stopped.

"Do you need…? Are you alright?" Patrice asked.

"I don't know," the woman answered honestly.

"Do you have somewhere to go? Someone to be with perhaps?"

"I can't remember. I have this address. But I've gotten turned around. It's my son's, I think." The old woman held up a piece of paper.

"We're going the way of this address. Would you like to walk with us?"

"You could go be with your son?" Patrice added.

"That would be nice, I think. Family is important, isn't it."

"It is," Patrice agreed, "especially at times like these." They helped the woman gingerly to her feet. She had no baggage they could see.

"Times like these?" the woman asked.

Patrice and Deval walked, the older woman being supported between them. Five blocks further on, they came to the house named in the address. In the driveway, a man and woman loaded boxes into an SUV that already had two children in car seats inside.

"Mom!" the man called when he saw Patrice and Deval, his mother between them. "Marie and I were on our way to come get you!" To the two teens beside his mom, the man said, "Thank you so much, we were so worried about her." His wife came over and stood beside him.

"Thank you," she said before leading the older woman to the SUV and seeing her safely inside.

"Bless you, bless you," the man said, and he turned back to his work at hand.

"Bless us?" Patrice said to Deval. The look on his face told her he was remembering the same thing. "That woman!" he said. "She said that to us *last* week!"

"She was so calm, so centered," Patrice said.

"Right. Her. Where is she in all of this?"

"Well *she* said to go up hill, remember. It seemed so obvious at the time, the sort of thing you'd do in a flood."

"But she also said that we would 'get through.' What did she mean by that?"

As one, Deval and Patrice turned to look to the foothills above their city and the other cities in the valley.

"I don't know," Patrice said.

"We have nothing to lose really. Like you said, it's what you'd do in a flood anyway. Maybe we'll get more information along the way," Deval said.

"Now we know where we're going anyway," Patrice said in response, and the two looked at each other, nodded, and cut through the yard of the son and daughter-in-law, headed, literally, for the hills.

"Take care!" Deval called as they passed the SUV. The woman, now smiling and seated happily between her grandchildren, waved and yelled again, as her son had, "Bless you!" With that the SUV backed out of the driveway into the quickly clogging neighborhood artery.

*

After they'd gained some elevation, Patrice and Deval could see both Distoria and Malanthron in the distance. On the hillside, among the travelers, Patrice stood out to Deval because of the bright pink back pack she carried. He had chuckled when she'd shown up with it. But now he was thankful for it. In a funny way, keeping track of her allowed him to feel he was keeping track of himself. That comfort meant more today than any comfort ever had before.

All over the as-of-yet still dry land, roads, and hillsides, people moved about everywhere, like ants. Some moved quickly, in a scurry, but most walked with heads bent, moving slowly with the heat. From all three cities, people of all ages, carrying suitcases and wearing backpacks, thinking the water was going to allow them to take with them their worldly possessions, now streamed up, out, away from the water, and up the hillside.

15

The villages on the hillside, filled with shanties and grouped-up Out-Citiers, had grown in recent weeks. Among them and along the Gates, Out-Citiers sat, foraged, or hunted small mammals in packs. Some were catching and eating bugs to gain the protein and to fill the void in their stomachs. Still others vomited as Tony passed, or lay ill in or near their shanties. One man sat staring blankly at his broken and bleeding leg stretched out in front of him.

As Tony kept walking, carrying nothing but a walking stick, he chanted. "Om-mane-padme-om," he repeated quietly. Around him he sensed the action more than he saw it. To his right, he was aware when one Out-Citier attacked a couple in their shanty. The woman of the couple held a water bottle which the attacker demanded from her at knife point, the knife being held against her husband's neck. Not willing to watch her husband die, the woman handed it over.

Tony stopped walking when he got to this man who'd stolen the water and had begun to drink. He stood before the man, hand out, saying nothing. The man stopped drinking and looked questioningly at Tony. After a long moment, the man, not knowing why, capped the water bottle and placed it in Tony's outstretched hand.

Tony then turned and walked to the couple in the shanty. Still wordless, he handed the bottle back to the woman who was more than grateful. She and her husband showered him with thanks as he turned and continued his chanting and his climb up the hill.

Tony walked until he reached a group of seated people. The seated people chanted as Tony did, and because they did, he set down his walking stick when he got to them. He took the hands of two of those chanting. The two stood then, and the other meditators followed suit, grasping hands and forming a circle.

In minutes, the group became translucent. Moments later, they had disappeared.

*

One of the men in the group of meditators broke into sobs when they arrived inside the camp. His were not tears of happiness though, for the man, alternating between mumbling and shrieking, called out, "Lies," over and over. "Everything they told me... in my childhood... about life... all lies," he managed to add eventually, around his heaving sobs.

16

In a meadow, far from Transport Hall where the chanters and Tony had just arrived, Anna, George and Gabby rode on horseback.

Without warning, Anna stopped riding and closed her eyes. Turning her face skyward, she appeared to the two beside her, to be listening. Finally, she turned to George and Gabby.

"The Keystone, the first of them, has arrived. Let us head back as more Keystones will be arriving soon." With that she motioned Shasta forward and indicated to the horse to turn back the way they'd all come.

George and Gabby turned their horses as well and rode along beside Anna a while before Gabby spoke.

"Keystones?" she asked.

Anna looked for a moment as if she did not understand. But she simply said, "Those who can help the others." She rode again long enough that the other two thought perhaps that might be all she was going to say on the subject. Just as they had decided they would only find out more once they'd reached Transport Hall, Anna spoke again. She added, "The Keystones can decrease the learning curve for others. They enable openness."

"If they were to learn that bias isn't real, that conflict isn't real, they could get through the filters. Once the falsehood that is "man versus man" is gone," Anna said.

"I thought it was only to keep out those willing to do violence," George said.

"Bias is violence," Gabby said.

"True, and all of it is false anyway," George added.

The two spoke as if Anna weren't with them and Anna behaved as if she hadn't heard. When she spoke again, she did it without looking at George or at Gabby. It was as if she were talking simply to herself. "Say the Gates were a metaphor," she continued, "for say Heaven, or Nirvana, then it would be like the Keystones were out there handing that to those outside the Gates – Heaven or Nirvana – overnight." She rode another four strides before adding, "The emotional impact though, on the newly arrived, from so much growth so fast, can be severe. The Keystones will need help. They will need us."

17

As William and one of the men who'd been with him in the financial district walked, directionless, into view on the hillside, petty thefts were rampant around them.

"These people steal out of boredom as much as from necessity," William remarked to his former colleague, Jonah. But before the colleague could respond, another man called out to them by name from inside one of the shanties.

"William," this unseen man yelled.

At that, the two newly-arrived men startled and were re-invested with energy. They now no longer walked randomly, but in a more definitive direction - toward that one of the shanty villages, and toward that voice. The speaker came out from inside his shelter. There was a cheer from several dwellings around them as William recognized another of the colleagues he'd jovially swapped stories with in what he was rapidly coming to think of as his, "old life." The other men, those who'd cheered, came out of the dwellings too. One of the men, the speaker, then handed William a weapon.

"We have been waiting for you," he told William.

"We've been hoping you would show. We need you," another man said. "We mean for you to lead our assault on them!" Here he pointed toward the other village. "Their alliance steals our food and injures our people."

William looked at both villages then thought for a moment. Finally, as the others watched, he dropped his backpack, raised his weapon over his head, and gave a tremendously loud war-like call. The others, taking that for agreement, raised their own arms as well and followed William in his war cries and loud bellowing.

18

The next morning, Anna sat again in the chair inside Transport Hall, Hala and Haldor beside her.

"The Great Departure nears," Hala said.

In answer, Anna closed her eyes. In a minute, they opened again, filled now with a different presence. Anna reached out, connecting through space with twelve different young, but knowing, minds around the globe. To each she spoke, personally delivering the messages in all twelve directions.

Faster than light, Anna moved from house to house, at one point existing in all twelve locations and the room, simultaneously for several seconds. Then, that work done, she was fully returned to only the room.

In one house, the child received this message, "Lift yourself now. Come to me now. You will bring your family here soon."

"I will go to Dr. Anna now, Dad. I will call to you, bring you, soon," that child responded before vibrating, lifting, moving through the unopened door, and into what appeared to be the sky.

In India, a Dalit child of seven received Anna's message and turned to his parents. He gestured good-bye, left a comforting word of reassurance for them, vibrated, lifted himself up, and entered the ethos via a pathway created millennia ago and lost to most of humanity. The pathway had a name, but even that, save to Anna and these children, had fallen along the byways of humanity long ago.

In ten other homes, around the world, ten more children of all ages, genders, ethnic groups and eye colors, became aware of the presence in their minds, of Anna's message. They felt the subtle sensitivities and responded. Ten children gestured to their parents, reassured them, connected to the pathway and were gone.

The children, moving in rhythm with the speed of that which they had each become - light, flew passed planets, constellations, comets, debris. They absorbed energy from the universe, each one doing so at a frequency consistent with deepest space, the same frequency inside themselves.

The translucent children came from distant locations, but moved toward a single location. Within a few seconds from the arrival of the first, all twelve had arrived as if through the hall roof and ceiling.

Each of the twelve touched down on the floor of the Hall. Each of the twelve quickly became solid again, losing their glowing translucence. Haldor re-entered the Hall and moved, as always, directly toward Anna, to offer the protection needed after so taxing an endeavor.

Hala, Hadar, Hakon, Haluk and two more Helper Classers re-entered as well. Each carried the requisite and freshly warmed robe. Each of the devoted Helpers wrapped two children in the welcoming robes, then escorted their two charges from the hall towards quick medical checks followed by sweet treats.

Anna however, did not rise as per usual, despite Haldor's approach.

"Doctor? Do you not wish to return to chamber for your post-telepa-port rest?"

"Indeed. Perhaps not, Haldor. I am... I'm feeling..." Anna stood. "Oddly, I am feeling... well, I'm fine. More than fine."

"Doctor?"

"Better."

"Did the children...?"

"They must have," she said. She walked around the chair in a circle, then still reflecting, sat down again.

"Let's do it again, Haldor. Let's message another twelve children."

"Right now?"

"Right now."

"So soon?

"Line 'em up," she joked, though the joke was mostly lost on her companion. "Oh, and we will need to bring in the young couple I spoke of, John and Michelle? Being nine months pregnant, Michelle will be in no condition to travel up to us, we'll have to go get her."

"Let's hope we continue to get the same outcome then." Haldor stated without emotion.

Anna saw the large, black man in orange for whom she'd been watching. He walked in just then, escorted by Hala. She waved a short, dignified, but warm wave.

"Ah, you must be Tony. Thank you, Hala."

"Of course," Hala said before turning and leaving. Tony looked mostly at the floor.

"I'm honored, Ma'am," he said.

"Thank you for heading up hill, you have already been most helpful."

"It was you, on the TV, is why I did. Head up hill, that is."

"Me?"

"Courage. You said ...things, and ...tolerance and... I ...just ...agree."

"I'm glad you heard me then, but you were the one with the courage, to allow your true nature to rise."

"Finally."

"Most never do. Most die before having met themselves. Always remember that, despite all the obstacles you faced in life, you did better than most."

"Thank you, Ma'am."

"But the question now is, you have a gift, and what are you going to do about that?" Tony looked up at that.

"Ma'am?" he said. Anna remained silent however.

"Well ...I guess I ...am," Tony continued, "...going back out there then?" At that, Anna smiled. "Helping more people to 'meet themselves' sooner, I guess?" Pleased, Tony's grin far outshone Anna's.

Anna stepped forward, still smiling. She took Tony's hands in her own.

"Thank you, Tony, thank you so much. You are only the first of what we call, The Keystones, but there will be more here to help you soon."

"I ...I can't believe ...that I have... something ...that I can give back... something." But he had to stop then, for the tears in his eyes. Anna stepped forward and embraced Tony solidly.

"Very much, Tony," she said, "you have so very much." At that, Tony laughed a bit, through his tears.

"Oh, and Tony, this increased learning curve will cause a variety of emotions in those you help. We'll send others to help you with that," she said, and Tony nodded, laughing.

"Seen a bit of that already, Ma'am," he said.

19

In transport hall, again the next morning, Anna and Haldor with many other Helper Classers, stood among four dozen children. The children were in various stages of becoming translucent, becoming solid, and being escorted from the room in warmed robes.

Haldor stepped closer, protectively, to Anna, still seated in the Transport Chair. Haldor handed Anna the glass of water he held.

"Such Success. Everyone is safe, including you, Doctor. Shall we stop now?"

"We just might be able to get everyone here who's needed, before The Great Departure. No, let's keep going. We'll bring in as many as we can."

"But, your health, Doctor."

"…Is hardly as important as this work, Haldor." Anyway, so far, so good. Besides, that's what you're here for. Keep one eye on them, one eye on me!"

Haldor hesitated.

"Go on, Haldor. I'm teasing you. Set it up again. Let's Roll!" Finally, Haldor exited to begin the preparations a second time, in a day that would likely see him repeating his actions many times more.

*

That night, Anna walked slowly along the ridge line by moonlight. George walked beside her. George stopped a moment when they saw a group of dancers by a fire burning in a circle of rocks, in a meadow below them.

"Dancing, George laughed. "Why always dancing? And by moonlight and firelight?" Anna took both his hands then. Playfully she danced with him, far removed from the other dancers.

"Is that your way of saying you want to dance?" she asked.

"Maybe."

"It's to be sure that the wild fire out of control, is still there, by the way."

"Is that so?"

"It is," she said and he pulled her close and they kissed then, a long, long time.

Then, they started walking again. They walked an hour together. But eventually, they ventured too close to the perimeter and the shanty villages could no longer be ignored. At the Gates, they stood, watching the violence and poverty.

"They seem to be engaging in petty, meaningless thefts, they seem to annoy the members of the other groups, simply out of boredom," George said finally after they had observed for a long while.

"It also helps, sadly, to strengthen their status among their own village members, at least, it does at their level of development," Anna said quietly. After a while, George spoke again.

"Even though I understand all that, and at the same time don't really understand how these people live with themselves, still, sometimes I wonder, how do *you* live with *yourself*, with the idea that you get to choose'?"

"Oh, we don't choose, George. They do."

"*They* choose!"

"Indeed."

"They... keep themselves out?"

"Yes, George, of course, they always have. That's how this works. Those people can't get through the filter because they don't have it in themselves. Sometimes people struggle even to see that they are blind."

"Why does no one tell them?" he asked quietly after watching for a long while more.

"Would it matter?" Anna asked. She took his hand, knew this was hard for him, as it was for her. "We have told them, of course, just as you have told your brother, William. It matters not. They don't believe us. They can't get there anyway."

"I can't... I can't believe it... Stuck. In their own minds... stuck." His sadness seemed to ring on forever, echoing that of all those who'd come before him, recognizing truth and yet, still unable to share it with all those they loved.

20

Though they walked through the night and into the day neither George nor Anna felt fatigued the next morning. Anna was in fact, already entering Transport Hall to begin her work as the sun rose.

Haldor entered the hall about a half a minute after Anna. Satya was with him. In the next five minutes or so, six additional Helper Classers and many more additional Protector Classers had arrived and stood, attentive, nearby.

Then Hala hurried into the Hall.

"Doctor," Hala called to Anna, "Doctor. It's Michelle."

"Yes," Anna said, "is everything alright?"

"I think it is, Doctor, but she's in labor."

"Goodness. George, would you accompany Hala, please? The child, she is one of us. Come back for me or Haldor if we should be needed."

"Let's go," George said. Hala nodded and the two hurried out. Anna turned her attention to the girl in front of her.

"Why don't you sit in the chair, Satya," Anna said to the girl after Satya had a chance to look around and re-familiarize herself with the space in the hall. Like most children her age, Satya carried a small, soft toy with her. It looked to Anna like a stuffed rabbit perhaps. Then Anna realized that it was the one Satya had found in her robe pocket on the morning she had first arrived.

"Me?" Satya asked, eyes wide.

"Sure, why not?" Anna answered, hoping her glibness might reassure. Tentatively, Satya approached the transport chair.

"Doesn't look fun," she said, and Anna laughed freely.

"What do you think you would do in it?" she asked the girl. Satya crawled up into it the large, square chair and sat a moment.

"You bring people here," she said matter-of-factly. Apparently, Satya already knew what the chair's role was, Anna thought.

"Exactly, Satya. You sit in it. You bring people here. Can you do that? Who would you bring in, if you sat there?" Anna asked. Satya closed her eyes and became so still that, for a moment, Anna thought she'd already left to bring in those who were pictured in her mind. But then Satya spoke.

"My family," she said.

And then, to Anna's surprise, the undaunted little girl did exactly that. She focused, vibrated, and entered deepest stillness. She did it as easily as Anna had at her age, and Anna was pleased again, happy to have found this one, this one other, on this planet, one who was capable in this way.

Satya's eyes slowly re-opened, with the presence of a different kind in them before she became translucent and transported through space under the power of the computer that was her own brain.

In front of her, Satya soon saw the cinder-block apartment building in Chechnya. The translucent Satya entered the building. She floated above the stairway, down the hallway, then through a door and into her family's apartment unit.

The girl's translucence wrapped around her mother, then reached out toward her father, pulling him close as they both became translucent. Finally, she found her eight-year-old brother, Alex, and wrapped herself around him as well.

Together, the four lifted then, and all of them shared in Satya's invisible state of being. As one, the four moved at high speed, transporting into what would seem to be sky, then through deepest space.

Earth, then the camp, and then the hall, became again visible, until finally, in a trip that took only seconds from an Earth-bound clock, the family was reunited in front of the large chair in which Satya reappeared.

Satya, translucent, was at once, both seated in the chair and with her rapidly re-solidifying family, in front of the chair. Her strong mind was not burdened by the sense that such a thing was impossible. Lacking the burden, everything became possible.

Satya's eyes slowly closed as she returned from her state of deepest stillness. Then, they popped open again as she saw in front of her, her brother, mother and father in the final stages of becoming solid again. Hala and Hadar entered then, warming and assisting the reunited family. Stunned and awed, none of the family had yet spoken. Satya moved fully to the chair before standing again and running back to her family. At the motion, the three turned, finally seeing their Satya.

"Satya!" her brother yelled and Alex ran to her, wrapping her in his hug. Their mother and father came around the children, hugging the pair as one.

"Mama! Papa! Alex!"

"Oh, how we've missed you so!" Satya's mother said, her eyes tearing up. Hala gave them a moment and then approached.

"You must be cold," Hala said, and she enveloped Alex in one of the robes straight from the warmer.

"Perhaps you are also hungry?" Hadar, who had come around to the other side of the family, said. "Here, come, let me show you your family's rooms." Hadar moved between the two parents and put one arm around each, to help warm and support them as they walked. Together, Satya, her family and the two Helper Classers, left the Hall.

*

By evening, everyone on both sides of the camp had heard the news. Christina and Anna sat in the cafeteria together, hearing the buzz of the news ripple around them.

"Doctor, the violence and intolerance against those like us continues unabated," Christina said.

"That is true, Christina, the news reports carry word of new incidences every evening."

"It has been said that, this morning, Satya brought in all three of her family members unaided," Christina said.

"Has it been? Then, truth has been spoken."

"So, she did? That changes everything, Doctor. Doesn't it?"

"That, Christina, is the very thing I am wondering about."

Anna and Christina looked out the window toward the other violence, the violence beyond the Gates.

"That... and will we be able to get everyone here before The Great Departure can be put off no longer."

21

Tony walked from Transport Hall. With him walked two Helper Classers and two Protector Classers. The small team walked into sight of the enormous crowd that hung just beyond an invisible line drawn seemingly, in the very dirt and rock of the overheated hillside.

Bravely, boldly, the enormous man walked directly into this purposeless mob without care for his safety. One of each of the Helper Classers and the Protector Classers stopped on either side of him, though they hung back just behind the unseen line. Tony stopped three feet into the mob. His silence, like a wave, created a space around him, from which the Out-Citiers stepped back. Then he closed his eyes and lifted both arms straight out to either side.

Without explanation, some Out-Citiers understood, and in silence of their own, they moved into the space behind Tony. All the noise stopped now, as still standing with eyes closed, Tony reached back behind himself and held the hands of the two Out-citiers nearest him. All the rest of those behind Tony quickly formed a chain of hands and closed their eyes as well.

During the minutes of silence that followed, another Out-Citier, desperate for salvation, ran up to the circle. He beat down on the shoulder of one of those in the circle and immediately, both Protector Classers directed their focus at the man. Without warning, he flew back from the circle and over the heads of many bystanders, to a point about twelve feet away where he abruptly met the ground. No one else attempted to intervene in the circles the rest of that day.

A few minutes more elapsed before the circle headed by Tony became translucent, and then disappeared altogether. It was as if only a second had gone by after that though, before Tony was back again, walking to his position just beyond the Gates from a spot where he had reappeared just five feet inside the Gates.

Three other Keystones appeared then, amid the crowd that was again, momentarily, loud. Tony, recognizing them instantly, smiled at the three newcomers. Then he addressed the crowd which immediately fell silent as he spoke.

"Everyone, everyone, we have three new Keystones. They can help. We can all help. Let us help you. Please, be patient. Wait your turn." To the three Keystones, he turned and added, "Ok, spread out, find a group, huh?"

Tony walked straight ahead while the other three took up posts at intervals of twenty feet. Then the process repeated itself with now all four Keystones standing solidly, closing their eyes, and spreading their arms wide to either side. Out-Citiers hoping to become In-Citiers, ran to stand behind each of the four. In a moment, the Keystones reached their arms backward and took hands allowing the circles to form. Minutes later, the groups began fading and disappearing. Each Keystone quickly returned and the process repeated itself without end throughout the day.

22

Beyond the Gates, out passed the point at which Anna and Christina now gazed, the shanty raids continued. Xeron and his twin, Xenon, led the raids that the women's gaze would have led them straight to, had they sufficient line of sight.

"They had a food stash, Xenon!"

"Of course they did, there's always a food stash, no matter how small," Xenon bellowed, unaware that he was being watched from far away inside a building on the hillside. He swung his makeshift machete as he yelled and on his downward arc, slit the throat of the mother who'd been hoarding the food for her children. Her three-year-old was safely hidden behind the few belongings they had managed to retain. These now, were bloodied, splattered over by fluids from the toddler's mother.

"Xeron!" called a raider from the shanty beside this one. "Xeron!"

"What? What *is* it?" Xeron called, moving toward the sound of the voice.

"This one, this man," the raider said, lifting the lifeless head of a man he had just this moment killed, "isn't he… from *our* village?"

"Aye," Xeron replied. "He is that. How did you come by him?"

"I... I killed him. I thought..." But the raider's thoughts were sheared off then by the booming, guttural bass of war cries. The two men, and all their compatriots, turned.

In their own village, not two hundred yards from this one, William's gang stood up from where they'd been crouching. The war cries continued, and grew louder.

And then William's raiders, who had patiently hidden in Xeron's village, charged. In a single moment, six raiders on the front line grabbed six villagers closest to them, and slit their throats in six acts that might have been a single, synchronized motion.

Suddenly, Xeron, Xenon, and all their raiders, realized exactly what was happening. They had been tricked. The men charged, with screams and bellows of their own, back to their own village. The rampaging men grabbed and killed, on their way out, two villagers unlucky enough to be in the wrong place at this very wrong moment.

23

Toward the end of the long day, the Keystones, hungry and wearied, their circles growing ever larger, they began to hear a string of guttural war cries. Tony, reappearing just then, heard them as well.

More chanters ran at the circles. Many Out-Citiers, spurred to action by action, rushed the circles too. Tony walked toward the circles. Out-Citiers shoved, yelled, and pulled at the arms and legs of those who made up the circles. A few of the Out-Citiers flew backwards after grabbing a shoulder or calf, as the Protector Classers awakened to the situation.

"Please, people," Tony yelled over the noise, "the circles can't get through the Gates if you keep…" but the Out-Citiers swamped him as well. "I'm sorry," he said loudly, you can't…" he pushed gently at the three who clung to him and pushed at his face. Firmly he removed a palm from his mouth and nose. "Please be patient, we will…" he peeled fingers from his bicep, "we will get to all of you. Please."

The Out-Citiers surrounding the circles flew from them as the force fields were put in place by the Protector Classers. Tony would await the arrival of another Protector Classer to give him help, now that he saw the circles were no longer safe.

✳

William sat alone, slumped against the invisible fence line that supported his weight without being seen. Desolate, he stared up into the sky and the relentless, unblinking sun. Slowly he pushed himself up and struggled to his feet. He wandered further from the repetitive noise of the group of Chanters.

"Should I chant?" he asked. He walked on. "What is it? What should I do?" he asked more questions. He turned to the invisible fence and grabbed at it hard as if it were solid or had bars, or anything at all that he could hold on to.

"Is this about God, is that it? If so, then God, you know, already, that I am not a good man." Defeated, he banged his head off the fence that is the Gates and turned his face again skyward. He had tears in his eyes.

"I wanted... I meant..." William started, "to be so much more... so much... better. It was the small decisions in life, so many bad small decisions... I... I meant... I wanted..."

Two from his faction, the two who'd enlisted his leadership and before that had worked with him in the city, walked nearer to him.

"There's William," he heard one of the men say. Hurriedly, he straightened up and swiped at an eye.

"Have you got, are those tears in your eyes?"

"What? Tears? Come on. No way." William stabbed quickly at the other of his eyes while he and his former colleagues moved away.

*

A hundred years before this, in the year 1984, the pre-dawn hours in the city would have offered relief in the form of cooler air, for an hour or two, before the heat of the day hit. In

2084, that was no longer the case in any location on earth. The sun would be up in an hour and the heat would pour down more then, the sun's rays cutting through what very little remained of protective ozone.

But, it was already sweltering when the dam burst that morning in the pre-dawn darkness, and water poured, as unrelenting as the heat, into Distoria.

Streams had become oceans and cement, in chunks the size of minivans, crashed through Distoria along with the water that had torn it from its moorings. The chunks tumbled and flew, rending holes in roofs and walls. The first houses in the downward line from the dam were flattened before they were flooded, the rest were simply flooded.

The yard where just a few days before children had played, carefree, now sat empty, wind blowing the swings about without the logic of back and forth. Inside what had been their home, a man, unrelated to the children, stood on the second floor. He rifled through drawers, closets, rooms that weren't his, searching for what had been left behind. He slipped into his backpack any item he came across which he thought he could put to future use.

That scene was being replayed in the darkened home where the father and daughter who'd lived there had shared a tea party in the front yard a few short days ago. Through the large front picture window, two more men, this time looting as a team, could be seen, sorting through what items would be, and which would not be, important in their future life and new reality.

"Don't take that! We don't need that!"

"It could come in handy."

"Food, water, cash, guns, ammo. Not much else is worth anything." At the same moment, the man in the first house and the two men in this house, turned, hearing a soul-shredding rending noise that, though they'd never heard it or anything like it before, they could identify immediately as the only thing that could possibly, ever, be making that particular sound. The dam had given way.

They, all three, looked outside. A car, whose driver careened left at the sound, slammed into a hydrant. Water then sprayed in a fountain from beneath the city. The car's driver got out and ran off on foot just as the looters ran for the doors of the homes they were searching. He, the looters, and those few who'd been more attached to their homes than their lives, were swept up as they ran in the ocean that descended where land had just been.

*

In downtown Distoria, the Red Alien no longer welcomed visitors to the Convention Center. Instead it now lay, broken into two large pieces, on the ground, each piece half covered by brackish water. Where it used to peer into the building, the top piece now seemed to be surveying the ground intently, staring as if to bore a hole deep into it.

*

Minutes later, it was the cement of the second dam, the one protecting the once busy city of Malanthron, which gave way in a heave. The cement boulders destroyed the first items they hit, then rolled and continued their devastation as water poured into the city around them. In less than half an hour, the famed clock tower of Malanthron was under six feet of water with cracks running up its side from ground to mid-level. The jagged lines looked violent in the burning sunlight.

Two men, red-faced and in the street in front of their homes, argued loudly, not bothering with their volume, while behind them, a home was in flames.

"It was MY plan!" One of the men yelled.

"You don't own the hillside! Any family can run the route into the hills. It's just coincidence it's the same route as your stupid family!"

"So, my family's stupid, is it?!" The man pulled his gun out of the back of his belt. The other man, seeing that, pulled his own gun too, from a shoulder holster.

"Now, Stan," the second man said, "don't be dumb, just think about what you're..."

"I'll show you dumb!" He shot into the chest of the neighbor with whom three days before he'd shared beers while ogling the neighborhood women. Stan's neighbor fell to the ground. Both though, were deafened to the gunshot by the rending of the dam.

"How's that for dumb, huh? Huh!" Stan boomed into the sky. He turned but did not register, that behind him, Distoria was already in flame. Nor did he register the closer sight or sound of thousands of gallons of rushing water.

From the ground, Stan's neighbor managed one last act while alive on this Earth, and that was to pull the trigger of *his* gun. Stan fell where he'd stood and the two men were immediately covered by the deluge, saved from their fate of drowning by what had become their even more ridiculous fate.

*

At the same moment, the cement of the dam protecting Antesapiana also gave in to the stronger force behind it and flew along on the newest of rivers toward the city below it. A few people were heard to shriek as the crumbling cement hit the high rises and businesses.

Once the tremendous wrenching, ripping, jagged tear into the morning was heard, the people inside the high rises shifted from normal movement into scurrying, running and careening motions. They jammed elevators everywhere, people's arms and legs getting caught in the closing doors as no one wanted to be left behind or be left to the stairs. People with backpacks and suitcases moved about in the hallways and lobbies. Back and forth some paced while others darted with less aim than they had hoped. Some tried to decide what to do, where to go. All argued. As the chaos increased, the struggle increased and people worked to get out of the tallest of the buildings before the raging river of water knocked the lowest floors out from under them.

One man, looking unusual for the backpack he wore along with his well-tailored satin pajamas, made a sudden arrow through the chaos. He broke toward the stairs. It was as if some spell were broken. Those who, only moments before, had been terrified of the stairways, now were terrified of not getting onto the stairs, of being left behind again, this time in the hallways and offices. The rushed and hurried push of humanity descended onto the stairwells and many went falling long-ways and head-ways down the stairs, being crushed further, under foot of the flailing, frightened mob.

In the street, those who made it out of the building heard sirens, cars starting, cars crashing - into other cars, and into buildings and people. They heard fire raging, water surging, people arguing, and shrieking. They heard so much shrieking.

Antesapiana had the distinction of being a short distance further up the hill, and closer to the camp, than Distoria and Malanthron, which though normally a selling point, now meant only that the terrified remaining population had the misfortune of seeing not only their own fate, but that of Distoria and Malanthron as well. Below them, both cities raged in fire and simultaneously, swam in the ocean the dams had released.

From all three cities, crowds of people, of all ages, carrying cases, boxes and bags and wearing whatever they were able, could be seen streaming up the mountainside like ants abandoning the anthill, rats abandoning the ship. Behind them, the cities in flames reached out like beacons.

It had taken only minutes, and all of Distoria, Malanthron, and Antesapiana were under water and any remaining stragglers who'd refused to vacate, for all their litany of foolish human reasons, were gone, killed before the pre-dawn had even given way to the dawn.

24

William lay in wait, just beyond the camp's impenetrable perimeter. Crouched low behind a rock outcropping, he watched. His two former colleagues who now never left his side, Jonah and Grayden, were with him. They watched as a grime-covered Citier couple in rags spoke to their oldest child. He watched as two smaller children cowered behind the legs of their teenaged brother.

"We must forage for you," the mother Citier said. "We will be as quick as we can. Please, take care of your siblings," she said, and the lament was in her voice.

"I will," her oldest child promised. The father Citier handed the teen a small bit of food then. Wrapped in cloth as if it were gold, the food caused the Citier to flash back to just the week prior, when his daughter and he had used a similarly small piece of food for nothing more than their tea party play.

"Take this, Dear Child," he said. The pair left quickly as if to cut short the cavalcade of tears that would have come. The oldest child and his younger siblings stayed there, watching them go, for a long time, standing just as they'd been. When their parents could no longer be seen, the oldest child carefully opened the edges of the cloth in his hand. He divided the morsel in two and handed half to the hungry youngest, just four years old. It was then that William and his cronies pounced.

"Give me that!" William bellowed as he leapt out from behind the rocks. The youngest was so frightened by the combination of noise and motion that she dropped the bit of morsel on the ground, attempting to hide again behind her older brother's leg. William knocked into the tiny girl as he grabbed for the food she'd just dropped and the force with which he hit pushed her backward roughly, and she fell. She fell in such a way as to land with her head against the flattest of the rocks, some of which had hidden William.

It was as William was grabbing the second half of the morsel that had been left to the boy and his siblings that the blood started to flow freely from the head of the now unconscious girl, onto the rock and then, into what was left of the dried and shriveled grass. The middle child remained where he was, never having left the relative safety of his brother's leg. While those two children longed to rush to their sister, they remained, terrified, where they stood.

Jonah, the first crony, looked at William confused.

"What did you yell for?" he bellowed before picking up and eating the food that had been dropped.

"I can't do this anymore," William mumbled. He looked at the bit of food in his hand and slowly held it out to the oldest sibling who took it hesitantly. The boy turned quickly, handed the food to his younger brother, and rushed to his sister's side, cradling her head in his arms.

William too, moved quickly to this youngest child, tearing his shirt off as he did. He wrapped a strip of the fabric around the little girl's bleeding head while her brothers stroked her hair and face.

The first crony, who'd eaten the food, and had taken only a moment to do so, lunged toward the boys as if he would come after them. The younger of the boys shrieked but William put his arm protectively in front of the boy and gave a menacing look to his old colleague. Jonah growled, but then shrugged and walked away.

Not far from William and the children, another Out-Citier approached one of his fellow shanty dwellers.

"That will cost you four food units," the filthy, balding shanty dweller said. He held a two-liter bottle of water just out of reach of the other man.

"I only have three food units for my whole family."

"Then," the bald man started to tuck the bottle away, "I guess you'll just have to do your business in parts elsewhere."

The younger man pulled a long blade from inside his now, loose-fitting rags. It was a re-fitted blade, re-claimed from another lifetime of use.

"I got two kids too dehydrated to speak. You'll give me that water or I'll gut you like a fish, old man."

Pulling his own impressive homemade blade from near where he'd tucked the water away, the older man said, "I'm not that old, young fool. Be careful who you misjudge."

"I just can't…" William started to say. Then he bent and cradled the girl in both of his arms before standing again and running uphill with the girl. "Do this anymore!"

Her brothers followed William up the hill.

25

Most of the Citiers, moving in the cooler temperatures of night, would take two nights to climb to the camp. Younger and healthier, would of course, move faster, while older or sicker would take longer. For Patrice and Deval, it took the average amount of time, but that was because they stopped to help several desperate travelers as they climbed. From these Citiers, they had heard whispers, legends about the Gates above them.

By the time the two came within half a mile of the Gates, the number of those who had not been able to pass through the barrier had increased both the size and the ramshackle nature of the two shanty villages. Members of the factions had gone among the Out-Citiers in the two villagers and shouted to them about safety in numbers. The factions grew stronger. They grew from nebulous concepts into solid being. Something existed now that hadn't existed yesterday. Along the way, tractability was replaced by that budding existentialism. Two tiny new nations had been born.

Deval and Patrice looked around. These people who had carried suitcases and backpacks, had, for whatever reasons they alone knew, not filled them with food and water. Most of what little food they had brought was already gone and the people now subsisted on edible plants, and at times, inedible plants. In each camp there were several people vomiting, sick from eating plants too far from the edible spectrum, or in fact, outright poisonous. Many others could be seen in the shanties, sick with viruses and injury.

Though it was night, there were many active people for the teens to watch due to the heat of the days. Even sight at night had become easier as human eyes had begun the inexorable movement of adaptation to their new reality. Patrice and Deval walked passed it all and came finally to odd lines of people in seated, chanting meditation. Beyond the chanters was a line beyond which no one seemed to be venturing.

"Why has everyone stopped here?" Deval asked.

"We may be getting close," Patrice said. A family, in their shanty, was attacked just then, as the two watched. The attacker walked away with a small quantity of food.

"Patrice, do you think, maybe, you know, that the Gates know... about my... you know, past?"

"I don't know, Deval, but you were a kid. You've worked hard. You're a better person since that joyride. We can only try. She told us to try."

Patrice noticed many of the children eating bugs as she watched, while older children tried to group together to catch squirrels and other small mammals.

"They are... are they eating bugs?"

"It looks like it," Deval answered. "But, some families must still have a bit of food left from what they brought up with them, otherwise there'd be no reason for the attacks."

"The attacks go on all night, from late afternoon on," a voice behind the two said. Patrice and Deval turned. A child crouched, peering out from behind a rock such that only his face was visible to Patrice. Though that face was covered in dirt, he looked to Patrice, to be perhaps twelve years old.

"So there is no reason"

"A few attacks are for food, but most are for no reason at all," the boy said, still crouching.

"Have you been attacked?" Patrice asked.

"No way, not me, I have tricks," the boy said.

"I'm Patrice, this is Deval," she said rotely, blankly. "Has it taken only days for the people to come to this? Only days to become animals and criminals?" but she wasn't really asking anyone in particular, just looking straight ahead at the chaos.

"The campers, from up there," Noah said pointing, "used to bring food down here. Enough for everyone."

"What happened, why'd they stop?"

"They realized it was causing some of the attacks. They brought box after box, left enough for everyone, right outside the Gates too. Then they tried handing out the food, like rations, when leaving enough for everyone didn't work. They even tried selling it."

"All that did was create a black market," Patrice said, guessing the result. The boy nodded, adding, "And food units became currency."

"That was when the campers just stopped coming," Deval said. The boy nodded a second time.

As the three watched, an Out-Citier in rags sprang upon the back of another Out-Citier who had been talking quietly with a woman who appeared to be his wife. The man who'd been talking then spun around quickly trying to shake the first Out-Citier to the ground.

But before he could clear the man, the man had pulled out a long length of sharpened, re-purposed metal and sliced the man's throat in front of his shocked wife who then cried out at the sight. Deval and Patrice also cried out and turned away in shock, alarm, disgust.

The Out-Citier jumped quickly down from the dying

man's back as he fell and grabbed out at the food morsel the woman had been holding.

"What else would they have carried uphill, and thought worthy of being carried, other than food?" Patrice asked rhetorically in her disgust.

"Why have they stopped walking uphill?" Deval asked then, shifting away from the violence.

"They can't get through," the boy said, and in illustration, he walked uphill away from the pair.

"See?" he called. He walked back to where he was. "I can go through, but they can't." As he spoke, another bedraggled traveler bounced off the filter and sat down hard in the dirt.

"The people on the hillside call it the Gates of Athena, but I think the name is just some legend or something. Whatever it is, it's powerful."

"But you can come and go?"

"Yup. I can go through. But my parents can't, so for now, I'm hanging close to them. Some time, I think, I'm expected to go through alone," he said nervously.

"No, don't be silly, we won't let that happen," Patrice said, "we'll be with you."

"But that's the problem. You'll get through right now. But it's ok, I'm ok with it, don't worry about me."

"We'll get through?" Patrice turned to Deval.

"That's what that woman said to us that day she told us to go uphill," Deval said, putting words to Patrice's thoughts.

"You think we'll get through, huh?" she asked the boy.

"I know it."

"We'll come back for you then, we'll come right here to the… fence, or whatever that thing is, and visit every day. And others, from up there, we'll all come, I'm sure others will."

At that, the boy brightened uncertainly.

Deval and Patrice looked at each other. They took hold of each other's hands and turned uphill. Deval looked back to the little boy.

"What's your name?"

"Noah."

"Well then, walk with us if you like, Noah."

Together, the three navigated carefully passed all the chaos, passed all the chanters, passed those meditating without chanting, and passed those who stood in groups speaking passages out loud from the Bible. They cautiously approached the area where these Gates seemed to be. Then the two new-comers hesitated.

They gazed questioningly at the line spread before this invisible fence, at the meditators, then to the boy, Noah, who hadn't hesitated and now was slightly ahead of them. They nodded to each other as was their way, and together, they each took one small half-step forward.

Nothing happened. They each moved their other foot forward to meet the first. Again, nothing happened. They shared again the slight nod and took two more steps forward.

Behind them, a man ran at the Gates. He slammed into the invisible Gates far to their left, with a loud thud. Patrice and Deval turned to see what had made the noise. They saw the man, on the ground, yelling words without meaning.

"He's from the city. He brags a lot, about how he used to work in finance with the leader of their faction, about how he used to *be* somebody," Noah said, shaking his head and kicking at a rock. Oddly, the man was only ten yards away from the pair, yet Patrice noticed that, his yelling was muffled to them.

*

In front of them, as they walked, two unusual people wearing what looked like one piece uniforms appeared suddenly. They didn't walk up or move out from behind something, they simply appeared; immediately in front of Patrice and Deval.

"Welcome, Patrice, I am Hakon," Hakon said.

"Welcome, Deval, I am Hala," Hala said.

"He.. Hello. How do you know us?" Patrice asked. But Hakon and Hala only turned and began walking up toward camp. The young newcomers, not knowing what else to do, followed. The yelling man from the financial district, was ignored.

"Young Noah, will you travel with us today then?"

"No, not today, not… yet."

"I see."

"Soon then," Hakon added.

The four walked uphill, Deval fist-bumping Noah for reassurance before going.

"We were told of your arrival, that you would arrive within two days of the water breech alarms. Come with us, we have made things ready for you," Hakon informed them.

"Told?"

"This has all been prophesied. For quite a long time. We are Helper Classers," Hala continued with the explanation. "We are always available to help with whatever you might need."

"You will need rest first," Hakon said. "And then, normally, lessons."

"Lessons?" Patrice asked.

"Normally?" Deval asked at the same time.

"To hone your skills to whatever level you desire. Except, now, well, things have changed," Hala said

"What skills do *we* have?" Patrice asked. Then, realizing how ominous was the sound of Hala's last few words, she added, "changed?"

"The skills your passage through the Gates proved you embody, of course." With that, neither Deval nor Patrice could think of anything more to say. The group fell silent and continued walking, the Helpers allowing the newcomers the quiet to absorb what they could.

As the four walked, a man covered in filth and blood, ran up. He was carrying a girl, cradled to his chest. She was young, scarcely more than a toddler and her head was wrapped in a blood-filled rag.

"Help me! Help her! She's hurt, she's bleeding!" the man was yelling. Hakon and Hala moved rapidly back down toward the Out-Citier who, unwittingly, had made it through the Gates. He was still running uphill as they came down toward him. Hakon gently placed his palm in front of the face of the child.

"She will need the Med Center. Will you be alright, Hala?"

"Go! Go!"

At that, Hakon held the child's hand and with eyes closed, both disappeared as Patrice and Deval stared. The man though, did not stare. He could only drop to his knees and sob.

"Will she be alright! Will she be alright?" he yelled over and over to no one. Hala rushed to the man.

"You are William?"

"Yes, yes. Will she survive?"

Come, William, let us go now," Hala said, helping him to his feet. "She will have an excellent chance. We must go now."

"Go? Go ... where?" the man named William asked, looking around. "I... I am through? I'm through? I..."

"Come. We must go now. Rest, food, departure, quickly." Hala walked up hill. Deval, Patrice and William followed.

*

Ten minutes later, Patrice and Deval followed Hala into a long multi-storied building with individual doors on most of the rooms, much like a hotel.

"This is the main dorm hall," Hala informed the pair. She turned down a hallway just beyond what would, in a hotel, have been the lobby. But a step later, when Patrice, Deval and William turned down the same hallway, Hala stood in front of a door nearly all of the way to the hall's other end. Patrice and Deval exchanged a look of concern.

"What have we gotten ourselves into?" Deval whispered. They walked to Hala, who, smiling, opened the door in front of her. The four entered the room.

"Whoa!" Deval let out a low whistle. Then he caught sight of an enormous fruit basket - and ran to it. He grabbed an apple out of it and bit into it immediately.

"It's real? Is it real?" he asked many times, even as he finished half of it without bothering to chew.

"The girl. Please, where is she?" William asked. Hala nodded. Beside them, Haldor materialized.

"I will take you there now," Haldor said to William.

"Thank you, thank you."

"Thank you, Haldor," Hala said before Haldor and William headed down the hall toward the Medical Center.

"This is your accommodations, Patrice, Deval. Please, rest now, you will need it for tomorrow is Departure. Don't worry, we will know if you need anything."

Deval's eyes now took in Patrice, as his mouth continued consuming the apple. She had laughed happily for him when first he'd bitten the fruit, but then she had caught sight of the tap through the open bathroom door, and had gone directly for it even while Hala spoke.

Patrice tried the tap, seeing water quickly pour from it. She shrieked with delighted laughter. She turned it off. She turned it back on again.

"It works, Deval, it works!" she bubbled, moving her hand side to side under the tap so she could feel the water on her dry skin. Patrice grabbed two glasses. She filled one, then the other, watching each with laughter as they filled. Then she handed one to Deval and drank the other one down till the tall glass was without a drop left in it.

"You will be well enough here until The Departure," Hala said.

"The... departure? Wait, we're leaving this place?" Patrice said. Deval moved closer to her, both to protect her as well as to gain comfort from her.

"Please, do not worry," Hala hastened to reassure them, "You will be going somewhere as well accommodated as this – and far safer."

"When will that be?"

"Soon." Hala looked pointedly at the rising waters beyond the window and at the violence beyond the Gates. "It will be soon, that much is clear."

"We are safer here than we were out there, Patrice, and whoever assembled this place has the money to have thought far ahead. Perhaps we'll be safer wherever she is going *from* here, too."

"Dr. Orlean has been able to generate a sizeable fortune, about that you are accurate." Hala moved to a linen closet and opened it. "Here you will find fresh towels, and a change of clothes in your sizes."

"How could there be...?"

But Hala had already left them, closing the door behind her with a click.

*

An hour later though, sleep had eluded the two, despite their immense fatigue. Instead, they headed back to the Gates. They were just around a bend in the hillside from it when they came into Noah's line of sight. Surprised, he stood and walked toward the Gates from the opposite direction.

Patrice stepped around the Chanters as quietly as she could when she came to them. Deval did the same. Each of the teens carried items for Noah and his family. Patrice had brought water with her, Deval, a small bag of fruits. Both things were hidden deep under meaningless wads of paper, in packs that they would take with them when they returned to the camp. As unobtrusively as they could manage, the two looked for Noah among the groups of shanties. They took care to stay near the Gates as much as was possible.

In the second group of shanties, they saw Noah walking toward them.

"I felt you two looking for me," he said, "it was just like when I feel the Helper Classers and Protector Classers watching for me."

"Well," Patrice said.

"Ya, don't know what to say to that either," Deval laughed.

"We brought you these things, Noah," Patrice said. "Is there a place we can go, to give them to you without too many people seeing?"

"My family is over there," Noah said, pointing. "I suppose our lean-to is the best we can do for privacy."

"That'll work," Deval said. The three walked in the direction the boy had pointed.

The shelter to which he had referred was only a few thin sheets of cardboard leaned up against some rocks. Despite that, both his parents lay inside the temporary shelter in the dust, coughing and pale. Their eyes were sunken and encircled by a dark gray coloring.

"Are you sure this is the best place, Noah?" Deval asked, "Perhaps there are some taller rocks or a stand of trees?"

"Trees taller than my knee have been gone from this area a long time," he said. "The only large rocks around here belong to those who used to follow William, those weird twins, and the stupid shanty wars," Noah added. "It will have to be here, or out there."

"Well, if it has to be, then it has to be," Deval said, taking the small pack from his back and handing the items from inside it, each wrapped in its own paper, to the boy. "I brought you an apple, a peach, a plum and an orange."

Patrice pulled the bottles of water out of her pack and handed those too, to the boy. "And I brought you water."

"What is it?" Noah's mother said. "What have they brought us?" His father leaned up on his elbow weakly and added, "Why are they helping? What is it you have, boy?"

"Thank you both," Noah said. "These will help my parents to feel better, to feel strong again," Noah said. The boy handed the fruit and bottles to his coughing parents who greedily grabbed them both. His father opened the bottle and guzzled down half of it without a breath, letting some of the precious water spill onto his unkempt beard and into the dust. Noah's mother ate all the peach in the same amount of time. While she did so, her other hand held the pear tightly in her grasp.

26

Anna walked toward Transport Hall. It was the early hours of the day, a time Anna had, in past, reveled in. It was the sounds of the birds calling out to each other in this hour that she had loved. Satya walked beside Anna. The little girl reached up and took Anna's hand in hers as they walked.

When they entered the Hall, six Protector Classers stood attentive, each hovering near the chair. Satya carried with her, in her other hand, the toy she had found upon her arrival, during her first moments in the Hall. Christina, Gabby, and George also stood in the hall, waiting, despite the early nature of the hour.

Anna and Satya moved slowly toward their friends and the chair. As they moved, four Helper Classers entered, escorting a line of children that included Chantel, who waved to Gabby. Delia too, the gifted artist, was also among the children and her lips shifted just a fraction toward a smile at seeing Dr. Anna again as she entered.

No one though, was to sit on the chair today. Instead, the Helper Classers had been instructed to form the children into a loose circle. This they now did.

"There have been eight more murders since Jake," Anna said to all those assembled. "Today is the day. Our Great Departure begins." A variety of emotions swept through the hall in murmurs. "We will bring in all the families today. Then, we will all depart together, immediately." There was no reply to be made to such a solemn reality. Anna moved over toward Christina to continue the preparations.

"Christina," Anna said, "please take Satya across the circle from me if you would." Gently, Anna passed Satya's hand into Christina's hand. Christina made sure to give a reassuring look to her young friend before walking with her over to the other side of the circle from where Dr. Anna now stood awaiting them.

"Good," Anna said when that was done. "Now take the one quarter spot to my left, please, Christina." Christina moved into place. "Excellent. Now, Gabby," Anna said.

"Me? But I'm so new to all this," Gabby responded from her surprise.

"New to it, Gabby? Are you sure? Hasn't it been with you, in you, all your life?" Anna said. Gabby knew this to be true.

"Where do you want me then?" was all she asked.

"Take up the three-quarter spot to my right, please." Gabby moved to the location indicated and Anna spoke again. "Indeed. Now, I think, we may be ready to begin soon." George and the four Helper Classers formed a loose, second circle around the outside of the first. Though George could not yet contribute fully to this effort he knew his line, the ground wire to this biological computer network, would offer protection. To that effort, he would add whatever he could.

"Chantel, shall we begin with you?" Anna asked, and Chantel smiled in response. "Tell us about your home, please, Chantel. Where it is, your family, your brothers and sisters, then we will focus on that and bring them here together." Chantel paused a moment, thinking, and then she began.

"I came here from Brooklyn. I lived in an apartment building there. My family is my mommy and my daddy and me. I lived on the third floor and I …"

*

Two hours later, the Helper Classers had received and warmed all but the last two family groups connected to the children in the circle. Hala escorted the most recently arrived family group, all wrapped warmly, from Transport Hall just as the second to last family group arrived. Translucent, they began to become solid again before the eyes of those present.

It was Haldor who moved comfortingly toward this family group. He had two robes with him and gently, he wrapped them around two family members. Haldor then escorted that family group from the Hall to first the Med Wing and then the Cafeteria, just as Hala had done for the family group before this one.

"You're all doing great," Haldor heard Anna say as he exited the Hall. "One more family for this team."

"Hakon," Anna said to him as he passed near. "Please prepare the next dozen children and bring them here to the hall."

"Of course, Doctor, right away," Hakon replied, exiting the Hall. In another few minutes, the last family group was hovering near arrival and Haluk entered the Hall carrying several robes, just as most of that family, translucent, arrived.

The father of this child's family however, remained passed out on a ratty couch in the living room of his worn but lovingly cleaned apartment. Empty beer cans lay scattered about on the floor around him.

"Haluk, will you check on Satya as you care for this family please?" Anna asked.

"Of course, Doctor," she said.

"Thank you, be sure that she is well cared for after all her effort."

Those of this family who'd just arrived were becoming solid now and though cuts and bruises could be seen on each family member, the first words from the mother's mouth were about the father. In her fear of the new, she called out.

"My husband! My husband! He hasn't gotten through. He's been left behind!" At that, her daughter left the circle. The girl approached her mother and took her hand. The girl stood like that, holding her mother's hand and looking up at her for a minute, then she spoke.

"You're free, Mommy" her daughter said. Startled, the mother abruptly cut short her anguished calling out. She stopped fretting and rubbed her free hand over their joined hands a moment, and reflected.

"I'm... free?" she said after some time. Then a smile formed slowly on her face and spread as she fully understood what this change she feared so, meant.

"I'm free," she said again. She hugged her son, she hugged her daughter, and then, accompanied by Satya and Haluk whose softened, knowing eyes moistened at the play of events, the reunited family members exited the Hall.

A moment later, Hakon entered the Hall, escorting into the Hall behind him, another team of twelve children.

"Welcome, Children!"

"Hi, Doctor Anna," called out one of the children from this second team.

"Alright everyone, now let's all circle up, ok," Hakon gently told the children. The children formed a loose circle and Anna, Gabby and Christina walked toward them to re-start the process for the second time.

27

There now were more than two groupings of shanties along the hillside. Most within the newest villages though, felt an interest in aligning themselves with one or the other of the original and now, opposing, villages. It was the hottest part of the day, about three in the afternoon, when just beyond the reach of the original village of shanties, a bedraggled group of disconnected Citiers arrived at the Gates.

Jonah, still longing for William, his friend and leader, to return, stood in front of the perimeter through which he could not pass, and yelled relentlessly at the new arrivals. In his hand he held a long, pointed stick he'd sharpened with a keenly surprising attention to detail.

Some among the newly arriving passed through easily, giving no attention to Jonah. Those who could not pass, stopped. Exhausted, many sat on the backpacks they'd worn. They too attempted to act as though Jonah were not there.

A woman among the new arrivals reached into her bag for her water bottle which she then held up to the lips of her son. Jonah lunged just then, so it was for the water that the woman and her husband assumed he was moving. As he lunged however, he grabbed not the water, but the ankle of one who, standing beside the woman, was passing through the Gates.

That In-Citier, startled, stopped and turned, attempting to shake Jonah's hand from his ankle. But Jonah would not be lost and instead of letting go, he bit hard into the calf of the In-Citier who then shrieked in pain.

A Protector Classer within the camp heard, then turned and focused her stare directly at the connection between Jonah and the In-Citier. In less than an instant, the Protector had arrived at the spot into which she had just been gazing.

*

In a hallway above Transport Hall, Hala, George and Gabby walked. The hallway's upper half was made of glass, making the scene outside immediately visible to those who, resting after the immensity of their efforts that morning, happened to be in that hallway, at that moment in time. George stopped walking first.

"Wha...? What is going on, what is happening out there?" he asked, but Gabby gently pulled on his elbow.

"Come away from there, George. Please."

Hala disappeared from beside them. As they watched, she reappeared beyond the Gates. Haldor too, ever ready for whatever assistance might be required, appeared beside her. Hala directed her palm at Jonah and then quickly moved it in front of herself to her right. At the same time, the Protector Classer also applied her focus.

Unwillingly, Jonah's fingers unlocked from around the In-Citier's calf. His jaws too, released. Jonah, not ungently, was moved backward, two feet. He was not hurt but was left seated while the In-Citier was moved, at the same time, forward two feet. The In-Citier, recognizing that he was in safety behind the Gates, immediately sat down on the ground and grabbed at his torn and bleeding lower calf. Haldor rushed over.

Hala faced her palm this time toward the lower leg of the seated In-Citier. Again, she moved it across in front of herself to her right. The In-Citier's leg no longer bled. Rapidly, the tear was healed and the bite and finger marks disappeared as well.

"Come," Haldor said to the stunned and staring In-Citier, "I will transport us both to the Medical Center."

"I will take care of things here," Hala said.

"Be in safety," Haldor said, then he and the new In-Citier became translucent and disappeared.

Hala stood just inside the Gates, waiting to see if Jonah, or anyone, would use the opportunity to attack. Behind Jonah, Xenon approached. Two of his comrades walked along with him. Jonah's associates were directly behind Xenon.

Jonah's mouth still was bloody but this did not impede him from yelling out to the watching villagers.

"This is war!"

He held up his sharpened stick high in the air and gave out a loud, piercing cry after his declaration. Then he stood and charged. He ran passed his associates who, uncertain, hesitated, as he did so. Then, sounding loud war cries too, they followed Jonah down the hill. Behind them and tight on their heels, ran Xenon's group.

The four men attacked the first two shanties they came to. Then Xenon's small band attacked Jonah's men while Xeron and another band of villagers, hearing the charge cry, rushed to the defense of the shanties, weapons drawn. Those coming downhill hit the first four villagers hard. Around them, armed villagers came swarming, also sounding loud battle cries.

Xeron and Xenon pierced their sword-like weapons through two men. More of Jonah's villagers, as well as more of Xenon's villagers, were in the swarm that had responded to the calls.

Intractability was absolved.

The war had begun.

28

Inside the glass-walled hallway of the camp, the two still watched as the world beyond the Gates fell apart.

"We must go. Now!" Gabby said with authority.

Gabby and George began moving then, but from Transport Hall, Anna telepa-ported them as they ran.

As the two reappeared in Transport Hall, Anna calmly continued giving direction. "Anyone here who has others left on earth able to get through, we must bring them in now. The war has begun. The Departure happens now."

Helper Classers and Protector Classers alike began moving with speed but precision, each knowing their role.

"Gabby, I would like it if you would be in one of the first waves of those departing."

"But why? I want to stay to help you."

"You might be able to provide extra support from that end, to help pull a few the last bit of the way."

"Then I will be honored."

"What about you?" George asked. "You'll be last, won't you?

"The very last."

"Then I'll be last too."

"I thought you might say that."

Action filled Transport Hall which overflowed with students, Helper Classers, family members, and Protector Classers, as well as a myriad of others rapidly performing an assortment of tasks in final preparations.

Anna and George stood among the sea of humans and activity. The Protector Classers, incredibly active though they were without motion, lined the walls by the dozen.

Anna and George walked toward the chair.

"Get the first five dozen lined up in front, will you, please?" Anna asked Haluk as she passed her.

"Of course, Dr. Anna," she said.

Tony entered the room and moved with purpose to directly approach Anna. Behind him, five lines of twelve people quickly formed in front of the chair.

"Sixty?" George asked. "Isn't that too many?"

"We arc all now going to one place, from one place," she said. "I shall do my best."

"Your best might cost your life."

"Then I will give my life."

"Ma'am." But it was Tony speaking, not George. "Ma'am, I'm sorry, but I'd like to go back." Any response Anna might have given was cut short by the approach of yet another. This time it was William approaching. He was escorted by Christina.

"William?" George yelled. William held one arm immobile against his chest.

"George? Georgie-boy," William said, but his low chuckle at this unexpected reunion was as exhausted as he was. "What are you... I see. Always the better of the two of us, weren't you?"

"I never thought... I was so worried you'd..." The brothers hit each other in an embrace. It lasted longer than any they'd shared before. There was not time though for the greater reflection the brothers desired.

"Did I hear someone mention going back?" William said, releasing his brother.

"I'm Tony."

"William."

"I'd like to go back."

"Then I'm going back too," William said.

"The Departure is now, right now. We're going," George said.

"Please. Ma'am, one more might make it," William said. Tony, looking at him appreciatively, nodded.

"You?" George asked, surprised. Then George too, looked on his brother with a new respect.

"I want to go back. I am not a Keystone, like Tony here. But I was a leader there and maybe someone will listen."

"I want to try," both men said to Anna together.

"Go, now, save anyone you can save. But, move quickly!" she added as William gave George a brief squeeze. "And get back here!" George called after William and Tony who were already moving for the exit at a dead run.

Gabby stood at the front corner of the group of sixty. Facing the lines of people, she held her arms up flat, out to the sides. With that, the chaos moved toward order and the noise dulled some. Christina and another strong Helper Class stood at the two back corners of the group. They too, faced the lines of departing people.

Satya approached and she too turned to face the people before stopping. But as Anna was about to close her eyes, she felt the tug that played inside George. It was the tug between staying here and going after William.

"Go," she told him without words. "Help him."

George ran from the hall just as Anna closed her eyes. She entered deepest stillness and began her subtle vibration. Then, with the help of the four who wrapped the lines, and the help of all the unused brain power left on earth, she telepa-ported the group. All sixty began their own nearly imperceptible vibration, became translucent, and disappeared.

There was a breath-held pause among those watching and then, a cheer went up.

"Quickly," Anna said to Haldor, "Assemble the next."

"But the effort wears on you, Doctor," Haldor said.

"Please, my friend, we must," Anna said. Reluctantly, Haldor complied.

Rapidly, five more lines of people assembled exactly as the first group. Anna leaned over to Satya.

"How are you holding up?" she asked the girl.

"Great," the girl said. And it occurred to Anna that to Satya, this might all seem like a wonderful game.

"And you?" the girl asked Gabby. Gabby laughed.

"You should go now too then, Gabby, do what you can there, they will need you." With that, Gabby closed her eyes and was gone.

Anna looked questioningly over at Christina and her Helper Classer who stood far to the back. Both nodded at Anna. Anna realized that none of those assisting in the transport would tell her honestly if they were being pushed too much, too far. She would have to keep an eye on them from inside of them. Anna nodded to another Helper Classer who moved into the now vacant corner in front of the lines of people, replacing Gabby. The lines now assembled, Anna moved forward.

"Alright, then, everyone, let's begin again in that case," she said. Those at the four corners closed their eyes again.

Anna did the same and in a moment, the five lines vibrated and were gone. Another cheer went up in the Hall.

*

Gabby and other Helper Classers wrapped new arrivals in towels and robes on the Space Station to which Gabby had only been once before. Other In-Citiers appeared, translucent, as those only recently becoming solid stepped away from the platform. More Helper Classers arrived with more towels, Chantel among them.

Beyond the platform, a crew could be seen, as if driving the station. The Space Station was however, quite stationary. Gabby saw far more species here than she had on her previous visit yet today she focused directly on those arriving and needing help.

In the next round of arrivals, Gabby exited the platform room with a girl of about six, Chantel escorting the girl's father. The group walked passed an infirmary, a cafeteria, a meditation room and an engineering room complete with labs. The reality of the size of even a single floor of the Station became quickly undeniable to Gabby.

Standing at the elevator, Gabby struggled with the size of the floor she was on. They entered the elevator and Gabby stopped. There, on the wall inside the elevator was a bank of buttons. On it were more than one hundred and forty buttons, indicating the same number of floors.

Three other passengers entered the elevator. The new passengers pushed buttons and the doors closed. Even as it began moving, Gabby's group had apparently yet to absorb the shock at comprehending the Station's size, let alone overcome the accompanying inertia because they had yet to push any buttons.

29

Tony and William came around the bend between the Gates and Transport Hall at a jog, hurrying to find one last soul, or group of souls, if they could. What they saw as the area beyond the Gates came into view though, stopped them cold.

Rushing up at the men were three dozen odd inmates wearing filthy orange jumpsuits. The pack of inmates was running up the last section of hillside before the Gates and every last one was whipping or stabbing a home-made weapon of one sort or another in front of him as he ran. Many Out-Citiers fell where they had stood while dozens of other Out-Citiers fell in with the pack as it moved toward the Gates.

Back at Transport Hall, activity screeched momentarily to a halt as everyone grabbed at their heads. The pain was intense, the coming violence imminent.

"Departure must continue," Anna yelled over the pain everyone was feeling. "You, Portia, Pietra, take the rest of the Protectors and go towards the danger. I will protect those departing. Go!" The group of sixty people standing in lines in front of Hala became translucent then disappeared as Portia, Pietra, and the Protector Classers ran from the hall.

"Hala! Quickly! The next sixty! Please!" Sixty more In-Citiers immediately assembled into lines. While they did, Patrice, Deval and George also ran from the Hall just behind the Protectors.

"The Gates! They must stay strong!" Christina yelled to Anna. "I can be more help down here than up on The Station. Let me stay!"

"You must survive, Christina. Go!"

"We will never be safe from people who think security is external. Not even one can get through. I need to stay. I need to …"

"You need to go! I will hold the Gates. Now go!"

*

Beyond the Gates by a few feet, Tony stood silent and solid before the onslaught. He ceremoniously extended his arms out to his sides. Almost immediately people ran to him and stood behind him. Pietra, Portia and the four other Protector Classers appeared beside him then. Behind them, Pietra heard George, Patrice and Deval running down from camp.

"Noah! Where's Noah?" Patrice yelled. Then, to her left, Patrice saw Noah with a man and woman. The three were attempting to fend off Inmates and Out-Citiers. She ran to them yelling Noah's name and Deval followed.

"Patrice! Wait!" Deval yelled.

The six Protector Classers created impenetrable fields then and sent them outward to surround individual Out-Citiers under attack. The knives and home-made weapons bounced off the Fields.

Tony, still in front of a large group of Out-Citiers, reached behind himself, bending his hands toward the group. The Out-Citiers behind him, realizing what he was trying to do, took the offered hands in their own and quickly extended the chain of hand-holding throughout the group that had formed. Then Tony closed his eyes. In a moment, all those behind him had done the same.

As his eyes closed to the world around him, Tony was assaulted by an inmate rushing up at him, knife held high. The inmate had been waiting for the moment Tony's eyes would close. Pietra reflexively shifted her impenetrable field, throwing it to a point in front of Tony and the group behind him.

Running, George could hear William as he yelled to the Out-Citiers, some of whom he so recently led. "Everyone! Please! We can bring in everyone! Please, stop fighting!"

George came to a stop in time to see the knife meant for Tony's chest bounce hard against an invisible shell. The knife-wielder, stunned and confused, lost his balance, stumbled backward, and fell.

"Go behind the Gates, Noah!" Noah's mother yelled. "You'll be safe there." From behind her, an inmate ran up on her as she yelled to keep Noah safe. He punched her hard on the side of the head with a fist and kept moving. George, who had been standing awestruck and uncertain, now moved. He ran between two Protector Classers and took their hands in his. At the same moment, Noah's Mother fell to the ground.

Noah's father, now being passed by the same inmate, tackled him hard as he ran, and took him to the ground. Patrice grabbed Noah's hand to pull him closer to her and farther from the fight just as his dad got in the first three blows to the inmate's head.

Without warning, both Patrice and Noah were suddenly stronger. They looked at each other, then at Noah's dad on the ground who was about to be hit from behind by another attacking Out-Citier. His weapon only bounced, having hit something between himself and the man, which he couldn't see.

"Noah!" Patrice yelled, "You created a force field. Are you… a Keystone too?" Behind them, Tony and his group became translucent and disappeared just as William spotted two of his former colleagues and ran toward them.

"I didn't do it," Noah told Patrice.

"Together," Deval yelled in answer. "You did it together, both of you. Here now, quick!" Deval pulled Noah and Patrice over, centering them atop Noah's unconscious mother. He joined his hands to theirs as Tony reappeared and ran back down from the Gates.

Not far from the three kids and Noah's mom, William, who'd been yelling to his former colleagues, got slugged by first one, and then the other of them. Another inmate ran up to the kids just then and he too, attempted attack before his weapon also bounced off, throwing him backward to the ground. The kids and Noah's mom became translucent and disappeared as the man fell. In a moment, they reappeared on the other side of the Gates.

"See, together we make a keystone!" Deval continued. "Come on, let's go back and get your dad!" The three ran back down to where Noah's dad still grappled with the inmate. Quickly they encircled the two men. They closed their eyes. But, nothing happened. An inmate, whose attack on the three, proved impotent, bounced with the reverberation of his hit, into a new direction, attacking another Out-Citier instead. Still the two teens and their charge did not become translucent.

"Dad!" Noah yelled. "Stop fighting, Dad!" Noah's dad stopped moving when he heard his son. He got slugged in the face by the inmate for his effort. But then, just after the punch landed, the four of them became translucent and disappeared from over the top of the inmate left behind, who was now throwing punches at nothing. The four reappeared behind the Gates, beside Noah's Mom.

Just in front of the Gates, another inmate ran at Tony whose size enabled him to hold off the attacker on his own.

"Why you wanna do this man," he said to the inmate. "Come on, listen to me, this isn't the way, man."

"Inside you were a leader, maybe. We were all in the same boat. Out here it's every man for himself, Tony."

"No, it isn't man! Prison or earth, we're still all in the same boat, it's all the same. Not here, not there, was it ever every one for themselves!"

He shoved the inmate backward then, hard, and the man fell onto his back and slid downhill. Tony stood, strong and tall, and again moved his arms out to his sides. Out-Citiers ran to get behind him again. Another attacker from a seemingly endless line of them, sprang up. Pietra's force field held, protecting Tony and his group as this attacker slid down hill like the man before him.

*

In a section along the Gates far from where Tony and William and the others held off the onslaught of inmates, a vast band of Out-Citiers bearing weapons shoved hard against the Gates. They worked as a unit, hitting it together in one motion. From where their unit worked, they could see Transport Hall as well as the next building closest to it. There were only a dozen Out-Citiers shoving and yelling at the Gates here, but without warning, one of them fell through to the ground on the other side of the Gates.

That man remained on his hands and knees a moment, looking at himself. He looked at where he was and laughed maniacally. He looked to the Gates, looked at the buildings in front of him, looked again at himself, and laughing again in crazy fashion, the man got up from the ground. He looked back at the Out-Citiers, stood himself in a sprinter's stance, and then, because he could and because he had nowhere else to go, he took off running up the hill toward Transport Hall. His maniacal laughter could still be heard by the others at the Gates. Suddenly the others crowded there realized what had happened and they too scrambled to push against the Gates, hoping for chinks in the mental armor that held it.

They jammed themselves hard through the small chinks which flashed open and closed in this area, then they followed the lunatic in front of them, up toward Transport Hall at a dead run.

*

At the same moment, up at the front of the Gates, Delia and Satya appeared beside Noah and his parents. "Anna sent us down," Delia yelled and the two girls ran downward to the Gates.

"But if you're here, who's up there with Anna?" George demanded.

"She's still sending families to The Station," Delia yelled over her shoulder.

"Without... without Protection?! She's doing the Transporting, protecting them, *and* holding the Gates together?" He looked around and saw Patrice watching him just as Pietra, beside him, released his hand and grabbed her head.

"Oh, my God," he yelled, "I've got to get back there." He too took off running up the hill.

"Hey! You! Over here!" Patrice called to him. George paused. He looked up hill. "We'll all get there faster this way," Patrice added. He looked up hill again quickly, then ran toward Patrice instead.

Noah and his two protectors were holding hands around his unconscious parents. George jumped in between Patrice and Noah and grabbed their hands.

"Wait! The Gates," Pietra yelled. "They've been breeched," she called. "The far corner."

"Breeched? But Anna's up there. And the families. They'll overrun the camp."

"That was the plan – to give them the camp! Just, not so soon!"

"To them? All this time? Leaving it to them, to those who didn't get through?"

"You didn't think we were going to watch them all drown, did you?" she asked harshly, moving fast, but when George just stared at her, she quickly added, "My God, you did."

She shook her head and yelled, "Now Go!" The child, two older teens and three adults immediately became translucent and disappeared just as Delia, Satya and Tony moved to the other side of the Gates. There, the three stood tall in front of the onslaught. Each extended his or her hands to either side. They then moved them backward to begin a new chain as Pietra sent the rest of the Protectors on, to protect the breech. She alone remained to provide the force fields of protection to the Keystones.

A downcast William approached Tony. Three Out-Citiers were with him. His face was cut and bruised. "I could only get these three to listen, Tony," he said, disappointed.

"Three is better than none, William. Get behind me with them," Tony told him and William and the Out-Citiers joined the hand chain behind Tony.

Most of Delia's group disappeared, but went only as far as ten meters inside the Gates before reappearing. Several within her group had not made it through. Satya's group too, disappeared and reappeared with Delia's group, to find that only about half had made the jump to the heightened learning curve, and through the Gates.

"We're nearing the end of those we can bring," Delia yelled to Satya. Tony appeared beside them with William and only five more Out-Citiers.

"Fall back everyone!" he yelled.

"You might be right, Delia," Tony yelled across the gulf between them. A moment later they heard the Out-Citiers from the vulnerable side of the Gates start to scream, yell, curse and shriek. Satya's hands flew to her ears and the Protector Classers let the force fields drop. They ran up hill toward Pietra who closed her eyes, lowered her head, and joined with Tony and William to get all the new In-Citiers up to Transport Hall.

Just before the group could depart though, the screaming Out-Citiers slammed hard against the Gates. Tony, horrified, watched as many were crushed between the Gates and the rest of the mob in the assault. One of the Out-Citiers fell through at a spot where the Gates should have been, as they watched. He fell to his knees, then suddenly looked up at Tony and the others, a beseeching look of fear on his face.

"The Gates have been released," Pietra yelled.

The Out-Citier on his knees heard the terrific noise as dozens of desperate Out-Citiers crashed through spots where moments before they'd been held back. A look of terror was the last thing Tony saw of the man before he was crushed beneath the stampede. Tony and Pietra grabbed hands with William and closed their eyes. William was about to close his eyes too, when he saw Satya fall. Without a moment's thought, he dropped the hands he held and ran headlong uphill at the exhausted, worn out child. He hoped he would reach her in time.

The stampeding got louder, heavier behind him as he ran. Tony started up toward William and the girl and her group then too.

"Stop! Tony!" Pietra stayed Tony's motion with the message in her tone. He looked at her. "Now we need to help them *from here*!"

William grabbed the limp girl up, just as the stampede came down over him. He rolled, protecting the child with his body. But the crowd grabbed up his feet and pulled, dragging him along behind them. Tony, alarmed, could no longer see him.

But Tony needed to focus his attention where he was and in a moment, he and Pietra and both his group and Satya's, were gone.

He was back again in a single second and looked quickly around him. He looked to Pietra, then at one unmoving body among the chaos and the mob, and then another, before he found what Pietra protected. William, bloodied and cut, lay half-hidden behind some boulders. Satya, unconscious, was with him. Tony took William's limp hand in one of his own and Satya's in the other. In a moment, he had gone again, William and little Satya with him.

*

Out-Citiers stormed through the land so recently vacated by the Messengers that several even stumbled at the lack of the impact they had been expecting. Those who stumbled, fell, and those who fell, became trampled amid the fear, the chaos, and the momentum of action.

The rest carried on, the mob never slowing.

30

The last family member group of sixty was being lined up in Transport Hall. At the same time, George and Noah, Patrice and Deval entered the Hall at a run.

Also at the same time, but from the other side of the Hall, a crash was heard. It was the first dozen Out-Citiers, running up from the hole they had found. Breaking through the doors, they had kept on, moving into the Hall. Though they'd never been in the Hall and had no way of knowing where they should go, or what they should do, the Out-Citiers, yelling and screaming and shrieking, ran dead at the sixty calm, standing family members.

"No!" George yelled from across the room as he ran to protect those departing. The sixty became translucent and disappeared a split second before he could reach them. As the sprinting Out-Citiers faltered though, and looked around, Anna fainted, and fell to the floor, and George realized he had a different problem on his hands now, despite that the last family group was safe.

He realized this at the same moment the Out-Citiers realized there was a new source available for their aggression. As one, the group turned and ran at Anna.

George saw the way a seasoned athlete sees, and ran to where the group was going to be before they knew they were going to be there. He got to Anna and cradled her body in his arms, prepared to protect her with only his own body if he had to.

He hadn't stopped to see what the others might be doing, he had just run. But now, cradling Anna, he first felt and then recognized, Gabby beside him. Noah, with Patrice and Deval, were also directly behind them. The three quickly moved to join with Gabby, forming a circle around Anna and George. Before they could join hands, Out-Citiers, slashing, punching, kicking, were on them. Patrice jolted forward as she was slashed hard across the back.

Delia, the farthest from the melee, saw Anna cradled in George's lap. She saw Patrice's back, the blood, and the knife that had caused it, and suddenly Delia's voice bellowed forth. Heard above all else, all noise and chaos, in the room, she screamed.

"Get away from her!"

Delia moved her arms in a fury. Throwing first one palm and then the other toward one of the pack and pulling it back – with an Out-Citier flying forcefully away from Anna, across the room, and into a wall with each retracted palm. The girl, furious at the thought of Anna injured, threw her palms forward again, and again, and again. Now nearly all the Out-Citiers had been thrown forcefully from Anna and the group.

Tony and Pietra, with the injured William and Satya, reappeared in the hall while the girl was feverish to protect Anna and the others.

"Go," yelled Pietra to Tony. With Pietra protecting their injured friends, Tony ran. Unsure what he was seeing, he ran anyway. Then comprehension dawning, he moved directly for Delia, grabbed her up in a single, large arm, and without losing pace continued toward Anna and the others as dozens more Out-Citiers swarmed in.

Pietra, still offering protection to William and the fallen Messenger, fell herself, to first one knee, and then to both as the swarm descended. Then she too, passed into unconsciousness.

"Pietra!" Tony yelled.

It was then that Gabby understood. Her full capacity recognized, she lifted, unaware, from the floor. She hovered just a few feet above these people who were for her, a family only so very recently found. All sound went from her. In a silence existing only for her, she acted.

Without moving from where she hovered, she caused, in concert, every other being in the hall to be moved.

As one, each of the dozens of Out-Citiers froze and lifted into the air of the hall. At the same time, the unconscious three became translucent and lifted from the floor. Anna, and the group protecting her, began to vibrate before they too, were lifted and held, solidly, just exactly where Gabby wanted them held. With a wave of one hand, the littlest Empath and the two who had protected her, were gone. A wave of Gabby's other hand and Anna's protective group too, had been telepa-ported to the Station.

Her family safe, Gabby lowered the Out-Citiers carefully. Then she allowed them to drop the remaining distance to the floor as she let go and followed those she loved to the Station.

*

At the station, George, still cradling Anna, looked quickly around for Gabby. Relief came when he saw her re-appear, his concern shifting immediately back to Anna and the other four in their group in need of medical attention.

*

Outside Transport Hall, as the first Out-Citiers had broken down its doors, a charge cry could be heard from the land south of where the Gates had been. As Anna fainted, the Gates were released, and they fell completely. The Out-Citiers, thinking themselves triumphant, stormed the camp, cries of success as well as cries of war.

The next set of doors, after those of Transport Hall, to be torn from their hinges, echoed across the camp, bomb-like. Suddenly, Jonah's face appeared and the rest of him burst through the space where moments before, the door had been.

Xeron burst into the hall at the other end, breaking in through a window that loudly shattered on the floor as he jumped in.

Jonah's two lead compatriots followed him into the Hall at this end, while Xeron's men followed *him* in through the window he'd broken out, at the other end. The men met in the middle, weapons drawn. More men followed, in each direction, and they too, all waved home-made weapons held out aggressively before them, eager for the fight.

*

In the cafeteria, minutes later, more doors fell, more window glass broke and shattered on the floors or ground below them. Out-Citiers, filthy and starving, swarmed in. Like worms through dirt, the Out-Citiers crawled all over the cabinets, the pantries, the tables. They covered all the ground the cafeteria had to offer them before moving on.

Tearing as they went, grabbing and shoving, the Out-Citiers consumed everything in their path and every morsel that could be found, stuffing anything looking edible, into their mouths, and swallowing.

31

George stood at the window of Anna's room in the Medical Wing of this Space Station number V1.0651, which he had yet to take the opportunity to explore. He had already come to think affectionately of this station, unknown to him until he had visited it himself just last week, as *Babylon.*

While he waited, the others had come by. Tony and Gabby shared information they had learned with him as they tried to offer comfort. It was they who'd explained that the station was a result of research by many species.

But when the many visitors had each gone again, George looked out at the stars instead of exploring what would, temporarily be his home. Thinking and waiting, he gazed outwardly. He was standing that way when, three earth days in, Anna stirred.

He turned sharply at the sound he'd been awaiting for what had felt like a lifetime. Then he took a deep breath in and moved to her bedside.

"Hey, you," he said softly, as her eyes fluttered open, "welcome back."

She looked around, taking in her location, and the situation.

"You could have died you know," he reprimanded her gently. He'd meant to wait before he brought that up, but it tumbled from him instead. "Taking on the whole telepa-port process, the protection, *and* holding the Gates. What were you thinking?" His voice though was gentle.

"I'm fine, George," she said as she sat up at a slight incline. Her voice was weak. Still, she joked softly with him, "Takes more than a Great Departure and the overrun of a city to bring me down," she said. Then she closed her eyes again. George chuckled at that and at his happiness to have her back in any form, weak or no.

"The doctors were so unsure. You let yourself get so weak, so depleted."

If two medical personnel hadn't walked in just then, Anna would have had no response anyway. What he said was true and she knew it.

"We heard the monitors. Good to see you're awake," the doctor-like being said. Passing a device just above her body from head to toe, the doctor lightly reprimanded her, "You gave us all a good scare." Then more gently still, added, "Even a species measuring their lifespan in millennia can die, you know." In answer, Anna smiled weakly up at him.

"We'll be back in what would be to you, about half of an earth hour," the doctor said to George. Then he and the staff member with him, departed.

"It's just about getting more rest now, I hope," George said.

I've been "resting" for three days now. I think I'm good," she said and tried to laugh. It stopped at a quiet bark instead though. She shifted gears.

"What were you thinking about, in your own little thoughtful spot over there?" she asked, her voice beginning to grow thin, needing sleep. George looked at the window.

"I don't know, just... about... the camp." He moved a step back toward the window again, only halfway from her bed though, not wanting to get too far away.

"They… they'll keep fighting, won't they? In just three days, more than half are already dead. They're dead, even though you left enough resources for all of them."

"There have always been," Anna weakly said, "resources enough for all. War was never necessary."

"They'll all be dead soon. In a matter of days. It's all so damned unnecessary." He looked over at her, saw she'd gone back to sleep and turned back to look out the window again, at the vastness of what is possible in life.

"So damned unnecessary," he said to himself.

~Also by the Author~

NOVELS

The God Seed and The Dalai Lama's Wife

N'Athenia: Book II, The Empath Series

I, Ngwamba Mae

The Dance of 10,000 Years

Cakes & Ale

SCREENPLAYS & TV

Dancing Backward in High Heels

Driver Wanted

Salem's Revenge

The Ancients

Anguilla Rocks

Code Games

The Widowed Wives' Club

Magdalena's Children

The Cult of Horus

MEMOIR & MORE

Grace & Beauty: A Sliver of Memoir

Cold War Teens